✗ FEB 19 2008

W9-BXU-696

SPRINGDALE PUBLIC LIBRARY
405 South Pleasant
Springdale, Arkansas 72764

The Voyage of the
Short Serpent

The Voyage of the

Short Serpent

∨ A NOVEL ∨

Bernard du Boucheron

Translated from the French by Hester Velmans

OVERLOOK DUCKWORTH
Woodstock ⌐ New York ⌐ London

SPRINGDALE PUBLIC LIBRARY
405 South Pleasant
Springdale, Arkansas 72764

This edition first published in the United States in 2008 by
The Overlook Press, Peter Mayer Publishers, Inc.
Woodstock & New York

WOODSTOCK:
One Overlook Drive
Woodstock, NY 12498
www.overlookpress.com
[for individual orders, bulk and special sales, contact our Woodstock office]

NEW YORK:
141 Wooster Street
New York, NY 10012

Copyright © 2004 by Bernard du Boucheron
Translation copyright © 2008 by Hester Velmans

All rights reserved. No part of this publication may be reproduced or
transmitted in any form or by any means, electronic or mechanical,
including photocopy, recording, or any information storage and retrieval
system now known or to be invented, without permission in writing from the
publisher, except by a reviewer who wishes to quote brief passages in connection
with a review written for inclusion in a magazine, newspaper, or broadcast.

Cataloging-in-Publication Data is available from the Library of Congress

Book design and type formatting by Bernard Schleifer
Manufactured in the United States of America
ISBN 978-1-58567-920-1
10 9 8 7 6 5 4 3 2 1

*KNUD RASMUSSEN. MUT
ÁVANERSSUARMIUT
ERKAISSUTIGSSIÂT*

. . . mot vest, mot vest!

—NORDAHL GRIEG

The Voyage of the Short Serpent

Chapter 1

ⱽ

ᕼE DID NOT PROSTRATE HIMSELF.
He did not kiss the ring.

*Thunderstruck by the grandeur of the mission,
he accepted without a word the Cardinal-Archbishop's
letters of instruction.*

To wit:

To our beloved son INSULOMONTANUS, Abbott
of God's-Yoke, *Legat a latere*, Black Protonotary,
Proprefect, Inquisitor Ordinary and Extraordinary;
We, Johan Einar Sokkason, Most Eminent Cardinal-
Archbishop of Nidaros:

I. << It has come to Our attention that the Christians of New Thule, at the Northernmost reach of the world, for want of a Bishop in the Diocese of Gardar and for lack of priests for its once-numerous and flourishing churches, are in grave danger of returning to the benighted days of heathendom. Due to the extraordinary cold which for some years has reigned there, the ships which did once set sail from Our ports in great numbers conveying that folk's vital necessities are no longer able to reach those ice-locked shores. To satisfy the needs of the flesh, the commodities which they lack are wheat, oil, wine, malt, simples and other medicinal herbs, Frisian cloth for cloaks, hatchets both single and double-bladed, knives, peat-shovels, spindles and spinning wheels, iron, rope for navigation and for hangings, timber for dwellings and for boats; they have been reduced to consuming the vile meat of seal and walrus, and have lost the art of ship-building, so crucial if they are to avoid the savagery to which their isolation subjects them; said isolation having led to the loss of the means to escape it, a vicious cycle in which the Eye of Faith recognizes the work of the Devil; further, as regards the needs of the soul, infinitely more precious than the flesh, the disrupted seafaring has stayed God's envoys (who are likewise Ours) from shepherding that flock: there has been no prelate in residence in that distant land for fifty years; for want of a Bishop, no new priests have been ordained; nor, for want of sea-access, has any priest ordained by Us been able to attain those shores. It is rumored that, of the few gray-beard priests still living who were ordained in the time of the last Bishops, some are guilty of the crime of apostasy, and resort to charms and incantations rather than prayer; that, emulating these delinquent priests, great numbers of Christians have renounced their baptismal vows and now practice the dark arts of sorcery to the sound of the drum, hoping that in forsaking the soul's salvation they will obtain from the Devil some succor here on earth, either through the melting of the ice, so that ships may regain free passage, or through the increase of the sea animals, with the Devil favoring the hunt. We pray to God that they may all have perished in a state of Grace so that they might ascend to God the Father's right hand, rather than to have survived thus in the error of their ways, which, upon surrender of the mortal form, condemns them to the eternal torments of hell. Depositions from Iceland, given to Our blessed Predecessors, lead Us to fear that these abandoned Christians are given to sodomy and the exchange of wives, that father sleeps with daughter, mother with son, brother with sister, and that, far from repudiating the monstrous issue of such criminal liaisons, they favor them over the offspring sent to them by the Lord under the sacred bonds sanctioned by the Church — if, that is, the Church were indeed still able to perform such rites. It is even said that during the famine winters they sometimes eat the dead instead of burying them in Christian ground.

II. Upon the recommendation of the Order of the God's-Yoke Chapter, as well as that of Our coadjutor Björn Ivar Ivarson, We have chosen you, as much on account of your qualifications as of your circumstances, to betake yourself to that most remote part of the world to investigate the conditions of the Christian folk there and to offer them the comfort of the Word, while not neglecting to castigate sin, if need be, by sword or by fire, and to report back to Us upon your return all that you have seen and done, with a view to, if it so please and suit Us and likewise His Majesty the King, returning thither as Bishop and Administrator of the Diocese of Gardar. We deem your qualifications to be many and excellent. You are a Doctor of Theology in the Chapter of Lund; you obtained your diploma in Exorcism from the University of Uppsala, and were confirmed therein by Ourselves and Our Diocese; you are versed in the pursuit and extermination of heresy, witchcraft and apostasy, as proven by your efforts against the Moors and Jews, including burnings at the stake, in Spain, Portugal and all the Extremaduras of the South, whither you were sent to perform that duty upon collegiate authority of the Order of Saint-Dominic to the Order of God's Yoke. We are aware, however, that your charity is not confined to saving souls that are gone astray by cleaving them from the mortal frame responsible for their sins; not content merely to brandish the sword of vengeance, you have found ways to temper retribution with benevolence and tenderness, not only in receiving heretics and infidels into the Faith, but also in offering succor to their victims, by setting up charitable institutions to receive widows and children exposed to their influence, down to the very orphans of the creatures who clung so obstinately to their heresies that you were obliged to send them to the stake. Employing the revenues of your tithe ere giving Us Our share (for which We rebuke you but mildly), you have built and do subsidize a leper infirmary in Our Diocese, which you visit without thought of contagion, bestowing upon the lepers the kiss of mercy, wherewith to hound out of the mortal frame the sins that are the cause of its affliction; deaf to popular outcry, you even abolished the use of the clapper when these poor souls go out in public, after you yourself once donned a leper's mantle and roamed the streets of Our city of Nidaros rattling that instrument. We have thus chosen a man both of action and of doctrine, capable not only of compassion, but also of firmness.

As to your circumstances, we know that you have lived in Rome, where for many years you did serve Our Very Sainted Popes Gregory and Urban;

there you lodged at the Palace of Ascoigne-Mazzini, and enjoyed the friendship of the Count of Ascoigne, a French nobleman, through whom you became acquainted not only with the language of those distant races, but also with their customs which, so We are told, combine the utmost refinement with the abjection of the most repulsive filth; for they do not refrain from approaching their womenfolk when these are indisposed, nor even when they are themselves infested with lice picked up in the houses of debauchery, which in Rome, as everyone knows, are too numerous to count. Adopting these French customs, you have learned to enjoy fare other than the barley soup and salted herring so dear to Our flock; and, in the realm of the mind, not content to peruse the religious manuscripts of the Vatican Archives and those others you were able to consult at the Ravenna Catechumenate , you were guided by the Count of Ascoigne to read the Classics: Greek, Latin and Arab; since there exists no book written in French that is worthy of being read by a Christian. Even if that language had lent itself to being read, it is generally agreed that the French combine rigidity of rhetoric with flimsiness of reasoning, which together, We gather, shape their strange destiny. In the Count of Ascoigne's house there also lived a certain Venetian admiral who had less interest in theology than in the heavens (for the two are distinct, in spite of what one might think), and the workings of the firmament. It is from this admiral that, having already acquired in your exten-sive travels some familiarity with the ways of sea, you learned the art of navigation. It is that qualification in particular which, together with the merits and virtues detailed above, recommends you to Our choice. For, since the time of our grandfathers' fathers, the knowledge needed to attain the Northern climes has been lost in the very fog it was meant to pierce.

III.   And now, for all these reasons as well as others that shall, if it please Us, be made patent upon your return, We do command you as follows:

With the twelve thousand marks of silver which We shall have made over to you out of Our capital treasure or, if We so choose, out of the monies of Our tithes, you will arrange to have built in the style of our ancestors a vessel capable of crossing the great oceans of the North, past the Isles of Sheep, the septentrional Orkneys, and Iceland, pressing on as far as New Thule. This ship must be able to withstand the ice floes which, according to Icelandic witnesses and reliable sources, drift in the vicinity of New Thule; the icebergs which, we are told, break off from the main land; and finally, the great sheets of ice girding the land from north to south for three or sometimes as much as four seasons of the year; moreover, in the event that you should become trapped in the ice, the grounded ship must be robust enough to shelter you and your crew until the spring thaw.

You will consult the best and most experienced ship's architects, whom you will find in Bergen, in Stralsund, in Bremen or in Lübeck; but you will see to it that their predilection for large merchant vessels does not render them blind to the wisdom of our ancestors, who sought safety in speed over bulk; and you will also make sure that the High Congress of the Hanse does not take umbrage when it discovers that We are undertaking an enterprise which she herself abandoned long ago. We have requested that His Holiness the Pope give fair warning to His Majesty the Emperor, that in his supreme authority he will prohibit the Hanse from impeding in any way, and for whatever reason, the succor which charity commands Us to bring to those far-off Christians, particularly in light of the trading opportunity which it may yet represent. Upon consulting with an architect, you will entrust the ship's construction to the most renowned master shipbuilders of Our city of Nidaros, or, by default, of Bergen, but you will refrain from hiring any German, whether he be from Hamburg, from Bremen, from Lübeck or from Rostock. We prohibit this for three reasons. First, the Germans are wont to bark out orders harshly, in the military manner, and, given that this comportment is ill suited to the ecclesiastical balm which our business requires, it furthermore risks incensing their brethren shipwrights, who are not soldiers but workmen, and thus might affect the quality of the work. Second, if upon being launched the ship were to sink, capsize or break up as a result of a German master wright's poor workmanship, we should not have authority to hang him since We have no jurisdiction over the Hanse; third and finally, the ship-building art of our ancestors, lost in time but to be revived by you at Our command, lay in the flexibility of the construction, not in the force of hammer and nail; in the lightness of the structure, not in its weight; so that the ships skimmed the waves, rather than plowing through them; and if We should deem the architect, with your support and encouragement, to be sufficiently diligent and adept at his art to reproduce the brilliant craftsman-ship of our forefathers, such a shipwright, cut of a coarser cloth, might not be able to forsake the fixed preconceptions and lumpish skills acquired in Germany's shipyards. The ship will be of sufficient girth to carry, beside yourself and your servants, a Captain and his boatswain, a helmsman, eight oars-men to larboard and eight oarsmen to starboard, who will sit on the chests of equipment, goods and vittles, with provisions sufficient to last two months at sea. Should you be caught in the ice at such remove from firm land that you be obliged to pass the winter there, We entrust you to Divine Mercy and to your hunting skills which, together, ought to ensure your survival. You are to accept this risk, or this opportunity, bearing in mind that it is danger-ous to load a vessel too heavily if fleetness is to be the key to the success of your enterprise. You will also take on board a quantity of supplies for the Christian folk whom you will be visiting with a view to alleviating their misery; you will draw up a bill of lading in consideration of those needs which your charity and Ours aim to fill. This charity does not, however, extend to giving the goods away for free, for fear of pampering them, or of putting the notion into their heads that necessity and distress are sufficient grounds for relief. Good deeds must be repaid in kind, and, since repentance and a return to the Faith represent, We fear, but scant compensation, you will ensure that your goods are traded in fair exchange for such wares as the beneficiaries may be able to supply: bear or fox pelts, walrus or narwhal ivories, ambergris drawn from the belly of the whale, angelica for flavoring sweetmeats or as a remedy for illnesses, or other like commodities.

Upon your return, you are to deposit these items in Our stores against the twelve thousand pieces of silver which We will advance you, less such sums as may please Us to dispense to your religious or charitable institutions.

The design and the rigging of the vessel are to

be such that, even without recourse to oars, it will outpace the fastest ships of the Hanseatic League, both running before the wind and against it; for so did our ancestors' ships perform. Should a Hanse vessel attack you on the high seas, whether it be a merchant vessel or warship, you will resist in the name of the Lord, and you will not spare the lives of your assailants, for the Faith which it is your mission to save is of far greater import than mere commerce. Every man on board must therefore be armed, and each will carry a circular shield, as in days of old.

To attain Gardar, on New Thule's southwest coast, you are to follow our ancestors' directions, long fallen into disuse but rehearsed here below. In view of her allegiance to the Hanseatic League, you will not depart from the port of Bergen, for fear of arousing the Hanse's jealousy and provoking it to give chase and sink your ship. Nor will you depart from Our city of Nidaros, which is a nest of Hanse spies, and is moreover situated too far north to ensure a safe voyage. You will set sail at Kirkesund, in the bay protected by the island of Hvitsö, whither you will have had covertly conveyed by land or shipped by sea the supplies and provisions stipulated in this

Letter of Instruction. Thence you will stay a wester-
ly course, so that the North Star keeps at a constant
altitude of one hundred and twenty-four lunar
diameters above the horizon. If the sky happens to
be too bright to see it, as it is our understanding
might be the case after the Spring Equinox, you may
refer to the Tables of Oddi, Master of the Stars, a
very ancient authority whom our forefathers used to
consult to determine the sun's noontime altitude
when navigating the Icelandic route. The Italian
engineer who is assisting Us in this part of Our req-
uisition informs Us that between the Spring
Equinox and the Summer Solstice, as (and We pray
to God that you will not have occasion to observe
this) in the period between the Summer Solstice and
the Autumn Equinox, you must heed that, as the
spring progresses, the sun's altitude at noon rises in
accordance with these tables, from fifty-six solar
diameters at the Equinox to one hundred and two
diameters at the Solstice; and vice versa (God for-
bid!) from Solstice to Equinox. The Italian engineer
who has himself dictated these notes to Our sec-
retary (a discreet and humble monk from St.
Andrew's), instructs you to have a carpenter fashion

you a straight rule of walnut, as tall as yourself, scored with notches marking off the lunar or solar diameters — they are in fact the same — in multiples of twelve; when held at arm's length this staff will allow you to calculate the altitude. Should it break or become misplaced, however, know that if you stretch your right arm with your fingers outspread, the distance which you then perceive from the tip of your thumb to the tip of your little finger is equal to thirty lunar or solar diameters; in sum, the sixth of a quadrant measured from the horizon to the zenith above your head; the engineer has made this determination, even though he has never met you, in the supposition that you are of harmonious build. If the sun is too high, you will steer your vessel north; if it is too low, you will steer south; and vice versa in the case of the North Star . You will skirt the northern shores of the Isles of Sheep in such a way that in fair weather you will just be able to perceive them to larboard; next you will sail past the southern coast of Iceland so that the sea appears to the eye to be two-thirds of the way up the Vatnajökull glacier; then, never letting out of your sight the North Star at night nor the Sun during the day, you will push on towards New Thule; and when you feel yourself in the grip of bitter cold and you behold birds in the sky and whales in the sea, you will know that you are near. You will then follow the coast with the ice to starboard, until you find, beyond a cape with towering cliffs, the church of Our Diocese of Gardar tucked into the far end of a fjord. There you will fall on your knees and thank God, and you will hallow that fjord by christening it with the name of the saint whose day saw your arrival.

Upon reaching your destination, you are to introduce yourself to the Christian folk you encounter there and announce to them that you are Our envoy, legate, coadjutant, and inquisitor ordinary and extraordinary.

You will draw up an inventory of churches and their contents, sacerdotal vestments, religious objects, treasures of gold, silver, pearl, mother-of-pearl, amber or more humble substances, as well as their dependencies, such as offices and stables, horses, cattle, sheep, pigs and dogs, not overlooking — in case the practice has not yet been abolished, or possibly reinstated despite the teachings of Our Sainted Mother Church — the abhorrent class of slaves. You will count the farms, their inhabitants, their live-stock, their slaves as discussed hereabove, and the acreages of any pastures or fields; also the stores of hay, of fish and of dried meats, hanks of wool, shov-els, cloth and garments. You will count, in every fjord, the number of seaworthy vessels still capable of making an ocean crossing, if there be any left, although it pains Us to venture that you will not find any; you will count the barks and the fishing boats, the fishing and bird nets and lines; you will do all of this with the aim of establishing the tithe where such riches exist, and of dispensing alms where there are none. To that end you will have the balance of the twelve thousand Marks which We shall have entrusted to you; and for which the bene-ficiaries are to give you full receipt.

Above all, you will ascertain the state of the Christian population, in number and in spiritual fer-vor as well as the correctness of its religious practice, from the Rogations to All-Saints' Day and Christmas; the state of their morals will require your particular attention. You will investigate if wives are

faithful to their husbands, and whether the husbands stay within the bounds of acceptable debauchery; or if, instead of limiting themselves to fornicating with their neighbors' wives and maidens, they do
it with their own daughters or mothers, or even go
so far as to engage in sodomy in the winter months.
But you are to bear in mind that should the fiery
blood they have inherited from our common ancestors need seek some relief from the long artic night,
then censure must be tempered with compassion:
for virtue is a matter of season. You are not, however, to confine yourself merely to matters of the flesh;
you will probe their customs and daily habits, the
modesty or luxury of the clothing, the master's conduct toward the servant and vice versa, the cleanliness of the dwellings, and finally the ardor for work,
which is the sole guarantee of prosperity and taxa-
tion.

You will be as pitiless in castigating sin as you
are generous in recognizing virtue. You will ferret
out and punish heresy, apostasy, infidelity, neglect of
religious practice, perjury, gluttony, lusts both simple
and sodomitic, with such rigor that it might be construed as cruelty were it not inspired by a shepherd's

love for his flock. You will draw up, at your own dis-
cretion, but on condition that you will give Us a
complete accounting of it upon your return, the list
of crimes which you have judged deserving of death,
as well as the manner of inflicting it; but heed that
your compassion lead you not to excessive leniency.
For every offence you will determine the proper
manner of death: the stake, the wheel, the head vise,
drawing and quartering, the slow hanging, suspen-
sion from the feet or carnal parts (only for men, since
the female constitution does not lend itself to it),
immersion in boiling oil, or stoning, the preferred
method of our ancestors ere Christ taught them His
mercy; this barbarous punishment is particularly
suitable in the case of a return to paganism. You will
disdain, as too expeditious or indeed too gentle, the
use of poison, fit only for politics; the sword, which
turns the criminal into a gentleman; drowning,
which, in those climes, will cause the condemned to
expire of the cold ere he can experience the suffoca-
tion; or the beer funnel, for not only will intoxication muffle the pain, but it is also a waste of a scarce
commodity and abases the executioner to the vile
office of a common inn keeper.>>

Chapter 2

*REPORT ON THE VOYAGE OF I. MONTANUS
AND HIS COMPANIONS*

THE SHIP BUILT AT YOUR GRACE'S
BEHEST IN Kirkesund, leeward of Hvitsö Island,
was launched on the day of Rogation after the
snowmelt, to great public rejoicing. St.
Mamertus, champion of Rogational devotions for
farm and field, could not have dreamed of a more
auspicious occasion to ask God to spread His
grace upon the troubles and travails of the sea.
The ship was christened on that same day. After

considering naming it for the saint's day, I decided not to do so, for two reasons: first, because this saint was female, and any expedition sponsored by Your Grace could not without peril be placed under a woman's patronage; and second, the day was that of St. Prudence, and even though that virtue is certainly one a mariner should have, he needs it less than bold-ness and courage, which, lest one relishes the prospect of returning to port at the first sign of a storm, ought to prevail over an excess of cau-tion. I therefore chose the name of "Short Serpent," *Ormen Korte*, in memory of King Olaf Tryggvason who brought Christ to our father-land, and who in the Year of Our Lord One Thousand was defeated in naval battle, dying a heroic death on board his vessel, *Ormen Lange*, "The Long Serpent". Although Your Grace is surely better acquainted with this history than I, I thought it pertinent to justify my preference: in-stead of a female saint, I chose the name of a con-verted pagan.

Bold as our forefathers I did set sail, with

The Voyage of the Short Serpent

Your Grace's simple instructions, come down to us through the ages, ringing in my ears: from Kirkesund, leeward of the Island of Hvitsö, where we put to sea at Pentecost, I set a course due west so that the North Star did sit one hundred and twenty-four lunar diameters above the horizon, or four hand-widths from thumb to little finger. As we left Iceland in our wake — of its shores only the mist-wreathed crest remained visible —and already tested by extreme rough seas, a terrible storm coming up from the south separated us mercilessly from this course. The oarsmen bailed for four days and four nights straight without food, drink or repose; the Captain, the boatswain and I were obliged to lend them a hand. The cowhide canopies laced over the gunwales, battered by crashing mountains of water, were powerless against the sea's fury, and were torn off one by one as if they were but rags. May Your Grace forgive these unfortunate men; the fight against the elements rendered them so weak that were it not for my admonishments, they would have deemed they had not the time

to commend their souls to God. It was overriding
concern for their mortal frame that caused them
to cling to the bales; and Your Grace will rule
whether their failure to mind their afterlife
should be condemned, or rather ought to be pardoned, since the fundamental object was to preserve Your future Bishop of Gardar here on
earth. Next came a long stretch without a breath
of wind, a lull such as has never been seen in
Iceland's vicinity. Removed as I was from spiritual duties, I did attend to the temporal ones, tally-
ing our provisions and rationing the water by
strict arithmetical calculation; the oarsmen's
tongues grew thick, and their buttocks were covered in carbuncles. Sitting in their own excrement for lack of strength to relieve themselves
over the side, they toiled without cease at the
oars; the ship held the rank stench of a
Mediterranean galley. The progress we made in
gaining ground on the North Star and beholding
it move closer to the horizon was so scant, and
the seamen's suffering so great, that they commenced to grumble. I weighed with the Captain

the option of hanging one from the yardarm; however, not only did I have no assurance that such an order would be obeyed, but I also saw that the life of every man on board would be essential to the survival of all. I took the precaution of stowing their weapons under lock, chain and key in the large sea chest that served me both as trunk and as seat of high command. I reminded the crew that, as God's minister on earth, my presence on board was warranted threefold: by the ordination that had made of me a priest, by Your Grace's commission, and, lastly, by the fact that I was the only one adequately versed in the art of navigation; that without me or against me, they would succeed neither in attaining their destination nor in returning to port; that if they could not bring themselves to love me by inclination, they ought to do so through necessity. At which point I had the boatswain distribute to each man a half hand of ale laced with brandy, ordered a complete and thorough cleaning of the ship, and forbad them from relieving themselves at their oars; and they obeyed as good Christians.

But Your Grace will see that this was but the start of our travails. Another tempest cast us so far north that we began to come upon icebergs; and then, with the season growing late and the elements ever conspiring against us, thereby preventing us from heading south, we came to an enormous sheet of ice, which we circumnavigated, rejoicing that we had not foundered on it, ere finally becoming entrapped by it. By August the snows came. We followed any open channels we could find in this ocean of ice, trying to make some headway, either due south or west, but it seemed to me that we were rounding the same ice reef over and over, and that we kept returning to the place from whence we had started, in a channel growing ever narrower. The oarsmen's teeth started falling out; their skin peeled off in long strips; and now the torment of cold came to be added to the torments of hunger and thirst. Fear alone kept them from complaining ; only the loftiness of my mission kept me from feeling sorry for them or myself. The Captain and boatswain, hardened from childhood to the abominations of the sea, and exalted, even in their humble station, by the magnitude of the enterprise, had only words of deference for me and words of command for their underlings. It was at this point that we found ourselves without sufficient free water around the ship to dip the oars. In the middle of the ocean we had happened upon solid ground. On the verge of running out of provisions, we were now beset with fear that the ship would be crushed by the ice. And, indeed, during our first nights of immobility, despite the precaution we had taken to deck the ship with a sufficient quantity of tarpaulins so that the snow, instead of burying us, would form a roof over our heads, we could not sleep, so anxious did it make us to hear the rumbling of the ice noisily pressing in around us. I was counting on the ship's flexibility, neither pegged nor nailed but lashed together in the way of our forefathers, to be pliant enough to withstand this stranglehold. I soon had to recognize, however, from the cracking of the boards and the snapping of the cords and thongs that bound them together, that the ship would shortly be crushed — like a fragile shell of which we were but the soft fleshy innards. The danger being imminent, we assembled all hands in the middle of the night, in a snowstorm and in darkness, so that we might pry the ship from the ice and hoist it up onto the surface. Never since the Passion of the Christ has anyone seen such agonizing effort by so miserable a crew. These ordeals were but naught, however, next to those which followed, and, if any blasphemies were uttered, these ought to be pardoned and dismissed with scorn, if not with pity. In two days and two nights of toil, we succeeded at last in freeing the ship from its prison, and, upon taking down the mast, in capsizing it onto the ice for a makeshift dwelling. Sails, sea chests, goods and sundry effects were lashed to the topside, which was now the bottom, to create a sort of buffer between the overturned hull and the surface of the ice. These items were then firmly anchored by drilling deep holes into the ice, and made fast with rope and cord so that they would not be blown away in the wind. The ship itself was tied down with strong cable strung across the keel. These measures, thanks to which I am able today to report on them to Your Grace, were largely the work of the Captain and boatswain, the best and most ingenious men in the world after St. Joseph, who, it must be said, never knew the hazards of the ice. Notwithstanding their notorious lack of piety, Your Grace will agree that these seamen must surely have received their inspiration from the Holy Spirit.

I perceived that our lives here on earth would last only as long as the last cask of herring. The Captain and boatswain tried to catch fish by cutting a hole in the ice, as they do on the lakes at home. But the ice was already of too great a thickness; and being so far from land withal, for all intents and purposes out in the middle of the ocean, what sort of a catch might we have hoped for by angling through a hole? With death at the door, the two of them set out across the ice, on empty stomachs, in hopes (which I did not encourage) of tracking down game. They had heard said that polar bears sometimes ventured

far out onto the frozen shelf. They disappeared
one morning into the blizzard, never heeding that
the snow would obliterate their footprints, nor
considering how they might find us again if
storm or mist were to hide us from their sight.
The oarsmen, torn between pity and hunger,
begged them, on their knees, not to go, while at
the same time hoping that they would. I was
stayed from joining them purely out of obeisance
to Your Grace's strict instructions, and the obligation of preserving the leader of the expedition.
Shortly upon their departure, while I was at
prayer in an attempt thus to replenish our supplies, since for lack of wafers (which had been
stolen and consumed) I was not able to celebrate
the Mass, one of the men cut off his own hand, to
eat it. Weeping, he told us that since it was
frozen, it was no good for aught else. For the cold
did intensify our suffering so; the harshness of
our own winters and the dangers of our glaciers
are, in comparison, but the mildness of the gardens of Italica . The torments of hunger and cold
were now augmented by the stench of putrefying

flesh from the frozen limbs, too foul to bear description here on parchment. In my weakened state, I found the strength, as per Your Grace's instructions, to exercise my extremities, and thus did I avoid having to lose any myself. Alas, several of the men did not have such fortitude, and I was obliged to amputate more than one limb with the axe, sewing up the wounds with twine. Their groans tore from my heart what little feeling the cold had left there. I forbad them to do as their comrade had done by eating the rotting flesh from which I had severed them. One of them replied that the season was not Lent, and proceeded to devour his own toes. Compassion stayed me from punishing such blasphemy. The sailors were too weak to think of mutiny, and it was not difficult to restrain their impatience with the bridle of my authority. In observing the stars, I discovered that the ice that imprisoned us was drifting south, bearing us with it, and that the ship's position had shifted in relation to the heavenly firmament. Your Grace will find this hard to believe, and yet it was so: we were mov-

ing in a southerly direction whilst revolving on
our own axis, like the hands on the great clock of
Nidaros cathedral. After a number of days of
incalculable suffering, the boatswain returned,
but without the Captain. I at once suspected the
boatswain of having celebrated an abominable
Mass by partaking of the flesh and blood of his
fellow man, pushed to the brink by extreme need.
He fell to his knees and swore to me that he had
but followed the Captain's orders to save himself
by returning to our shelter, whilst the Captain
continued on his way alone in search of game.
The boatswain swore that he had neither eaten
nor slept for four days, and I believed him. I did
ween it a miracle that he had found his way back
to the ship; he said that he suspected that for the
entire duration of his foray he had probably
never been at greater remove from us than one
league. He had been able to find his way back to
us by following certain recognizable ice forma-
tions not yet completely effaced by the snow,
which he had committed to memory by noting
their resemblance to the familiar silhouettes of

the churches and mountains of his native valley. Well, I told him, then the very fact that he had found us without the help of a miracle was itself a miracle. He wept with gratitude when I offered him a morsel of rancid lard which I had been saving in my secret hoard. The Captain reappeared the next day, half-dead with hunger and cold, dragging the carcase of a bear cub behind him from some straps looped around his shoulders. This cub augured another, with its mother, both slain and left at a remove of two days' and two nights' march; it was our salvation, and never was a sacrifice (if Your Grace will forgive these mortal cravings) consumed with such relish. I distributed it unequally, giving the largest pieces, and the best, to those who were fit enough to venture out to bring back the rest of the meat: to wit, the Captain, the boatswain, and two oarsmen who, judging by their mien, appeared furthest from death and had all been spared the frostbite. The men fell on the raw meat with wild grunts, thrusting their faces like beasts' muzzles into the clotted blood. Accustomed as I am to see misery

in my ministry, this was the first time that I truly
fathomed the depths of privation to which men
can sink whom God created in his own image,
and it left me, may it not displease Your Grace,
with some measure of compassion for the vices of
the poor. I deserve no merit for refusing to par-
take of this meat; for it filled me with such revulsion that it was no sacrifice. The Captain's obser-
vations led him to determine that the floating ice
which held us captive was drifting toward the
mainland, and that we might hope to find more
game and, perhaps, make landfall; though the
land in this place might well turn out to be even
less hospitable than the ice. He mustered a team
of men armed with bows and lances to collect the
bears he had left behind and to continue the
hunt. I blessed their departure with as much
solemnity as I would employ were I absolving
them of sins which they had not committed. I
was haunted by the sacrilegious thought that our
salvation depended less on Our Lord than on the
agility of these men. They returned four days
later lugging behind them big hunks of frozen

bear meat and the carcase of a sea lion. That any Christian could eat such an abomination was beyond my ken, but hunger set me straight. The skin of these animals is lined with a kind of blubber, which we learned to burn by dipping wicks of frayed rope in it. The cold made us so ravenous for fat that we were torn between our desire to eat this lard or to use it for heat. Happily, the thought of the heavenly light, and the memory of the flickering fires of the Pentecost on the day of our departure, made us choose the latter. As much as the scant nourishment which the hunt had provided, it was this fire which saved us from certain death. It allowed those of the men whose entrails revolted at having to eat raw flesh, and who regurgitated all that their hunger had impelled them to bolt down, to digest something cooked and hot. Your Grace will find it hard to believe, but some even went so far as to consume another man's vomit. This practice was fortunately abandoned with the arrival of fire, over which we were now able to cook our vile ragout. Thanks to such sorry viands, we spent months placating our hunger without ever quite stilling it, and, thanks to two lamps burning day and night, which we guarded as jealously as any vestal virgins, we managed to cling to life, chilled enough to be tormented by the cold but not quite enough to freeze to death. The vapor of our breath congealed inside The Long Serpent's overturned hull, which was soon layered with soot-blackened frost. On St. Reverian's day we spied the coast of New Thule. A canal opened up in the ice, and I ordered the ship to be launched once more. Daedalus never built a more hellish labyrinth than that which we were compelled to navigate through that ice, the wind blowing southwest, so that we negotiated its intricate twists and turns but with the greatest difficulty. Once again we had to resort to the heavy work of rowing; the oarsmen's exhaustion finally became so acute that the Captain, the boatswain and I eventually had to take up the oars ourselves, thereby discovering that it is a noble thing for freemen to assume of their own accord the condi-tion of galley slaves. At least the exertion spared us the frostbite, our hands and feet being but meagerly shod in scraps of bear skin. Your Grace would have been hard pressed to recognize the legate, protonotary, proprefect and inquisitor in the lowly seaman, covered in scabs and rags, which I had become both for the common good and in order to accomplish my mission. After skirting the cape in open waters, whence from the south we were finally able to steer north, on Ash Wednesday we arrived at a place where the sea juts deep into the mountains, a landscape that reminded us of our native land. Then did we recognize that we must be close to those Christian settlements to which I was dispatched by Your Grace. Imagine, however, an immense plateau of ice flowing between the mountains and into the sea, throwing up peaks of ice ten times as tall as the cathedral of Nidaros or even spires of the Frankish monarchs, dead ships threatening all other ships with death. Try to picture, too, these fjords, blanketed with snow and girded by the frozen sea, a desolate sight where wind and cold allow not a tree to grow; and Your Grace will

understand why I came ere long to doubt the fea-
sibility of Your mandate, or that there could be
any Christians alive in this godforsaken place. I
even began to question the truth of the ancient
lore claiming these shores to have been a distant
colony of ours in olden times, and of the
Icelandic annals chronicling it, in which I had
placed my faith though they be written in such a
barbaric tongue. A hundred times did I hesitate
to make for one of these fjords and steer The
Short Serpent into the interior of that land. In
anguish I consulted the accounts in the ancient
pilot charts which Your Grace in Your wisdom
permitted me to borrow from Your chapter's
archives, but they are so vague that they are of no
help in recognizing anything. This turmoil of
doubt was augmented, in both the Captain and
myself, by the torture of false certainties: just
when we thought to recognize an island, a
promontory, or some other landmark, that entry
in the charts would be belied by the one that followed it. We put in at every place where the ice
permitted, and, upon restoring ourselves with

the hunting opportunities these moorings offered, would explore the environs; but we never met a living soul. We did have the good fortune of killing a reindeer, similar in every aspect to the animals which our own northern savages herd for their milk. We were hopeful that this reindeer would portend similar herds and pastures. But we saw naught but wild reindeer, scratching at the snow in search of moss. Our disappointment was scarce assuaged by the pleasure of eating a viand that did not stink of fish. It was on the fifth day of Lent that, in the freezing cold, we caught sight of two gnomes clad in oilskins which seemed somehow to attach them to small skiffs, which they maneuvered with paddles through the labyrinths of ice. These were clearly not our Christians, and we killed them with a couple of well-aimed arrows. The wind blowing from abaft, and the ice offering some discontinuity, I decided to venture in the direction whence they had come: since the gnomes had managed to survive there, albeit in the manner of sea-animals rather than that of men, one might hope that the lost Christians too would have found a way to subsist there. We sailed between two large islands, upon whose shores we thought we could make out some ramshackle stone huts buried in the snow, although there was no smoke coming from them.

We spent five bitter days wending our way up the fjord we had entered. The wind having turned against us, the oarsmen scarce alive, and the ice driving us into endless detours, I judged our progress to be less than one-third of a mile per hour. Our laggard speed may make Your Grace appreciate the pertinence of the name of our ship, which, I venture to say, did crawl like a serpent. Your Grace will comprehend the martyr-dom we suffered without the redeeming virtue it would have had if inflicted by heathen hands. Sinners, we were bitterly conscious that our gal-lows-like torment might redeem nary a sin. I could have pretended before God that my suffer-ing was in the service of Your Grace, in other words, His own. But He who can see into our hearts, and Your Grace, whose sagacity has made You skilled in ferreting out the heart's deepest secrets, would have seen through my inclination to seek safety in a port in precedence over the salvation of my immortal soul. Day and night was I plagued with doubts, agonizing as to whether we would find any good Christians at the end of this fjord to bring us some solace, not considering that I was thus expecting to receive from that folk the very succor which I was supposed to be bringing them. This worry kept me tossing and turning every night, although the jolts caused by collisions with slabs of ice, which in the dark the helmsman was unable to avoid, would have kept me up just the same. The list of sins my mind committed during those long nights is longer than the list of my afflictions. And yet, at dawn of the sixth day, some forty miles from the mouth of the fjord where the gnomes had met us and paid for it with their lives, we espied, to windward, lost in a desert of snow on the north side of a towering cliff face of rock and ice, a Christian house with a plume of smoke over it. In form and construction it resembled the houses of our country. To be sure, it was not to be compared to the magnificent buildings of Nidaros, nor even our peasants' cottages. But Christian this house doubtless was , built of stone, with two gables, a double-pitched roof thatched with peat, and a chimney. A channel clear of ice allowed us to pull alongside. In spite of the cold, which somewhat tempered the ardor of my joy, I kissed the ground of New Thule, giving thanks to the Lord for having allowed us to attain it, Christians among Christians. The day had broken, although the sun remained hidden behind the mountains, as it is always, until dusk, at this season. It surprised us, however, that at an hour when, even in winter, farm dwellings are usually coming to life, we saw nothing stirring there, nor anyone at work. A bizarre spectacle met our eyes in the paddock between the house and the shore. The ground was littered with dying sheep; they were unable to get up because the damp of their fleece, freezing, had pinned them to the ground. The wretched creatures were scarce stirring; thus paralyzed, they were no longer in any state to forage beneath snow and ice to stave off starvation and certain death. At the house a sight far worse greeted us. In the most sordid filth and foul disarray, ten corpses lay sprawled across the floor and the communal bed, their throats slit, so severely maimed and mutilated that it was only by counting the heads that we were able to arrive at the tragic tally. Aghast at this silent reception, I feared I would have to report to Your Grace that the pastorate entrusted to me consisted of naught but immortal souls, in the event, that is, that any of these cadavers had ever harbored such. Hunger, perhaps, as well as some other affliction, had caused them to grow monstrously emaciated, the skin but a paper-thin covering for the bones, so flimsy that a doctor of anatomy would not have needed recourse to dissection. The skin was covered in scrofulous black lesions, of medium size and thickness, signs of the devil, one might conjecture, or, in the case of the women and maidens, of incubi that had plea-

SPRINGDALE PUBLIC LIBRARY
405 South Pleasant
Springdale, Arkansas 72764

sured them as, whimpering, they drew their last breath. The lips of some were coated with yellow or scarlet spume; blood from the wounds had splattered the walls right up to the rafters. One of the sailors, whom I would have judged to be less sensitive, proceeded to add the pestilence of his own vomit to the stench of excrement issuing from the still-warm entrails of the dead. For the carnage must have taken place but a short duration before our arrival. The peat fire was still aglow. I noticed lying in one corner the horribly mangled corpse of a monkey, which astonished me, for I knew that its species did not belong in these arctic climes. A dog was licking the wounds of the dead; whether out of compassion or greed it was impossible to tell. We beat it and whipped it, and it ran off in the snow, whimpering. I made the men kneel at this scene of devastation and said a few words of the burial mass. Owing to the freezing temperature I forwent giving them a proper Christian burial, especially since I suspected that a number of them might not be deserving of it, if their deaths had surprised them in some diabolical deed; moreover, I wondered if our prayers would be subject to some divine computation wherein their inefficacy, in the case of the sinners, would be weighed against their benefit to the virtuous; or whether we might be committing a sacrilege in praying for the devil's spawn.

We explored the miserable outbuildings in search of survivors. In the byre we found naught but some cows with shriveled udders, and a horse with feet so poorly trimmed that its hooves had grown to an inordinate length and were of such hindrance to the wretched animal that it could not even stand. All were dying of starvation by their empty feeding troughs. We saw that there was no hay, which was confirmed by a visit to the hayloft. The most hardened of my comrades, for all that each had had his own share of woes, wept at the sight of a destitution scarce less extreme than their own: which did not, however, stay them from promptly and with nary a qualm butchering a pig, or, rather, the mere shadow of a pig, discovered in the pigsty next to the

scarcely less filthy human abode. They also finished off some of the sheep writhing on the ice.
They did not slaughter the cows or the horse,
since in the men's exhausted state, the weight of
these animals, although they were emaciated,
made the task of dragging them back to our ship
simply too arduous; thus, fatigue and starvation
robbed them of even the means to remedy it.
Then, in one of those caprices of the weather
which so frequently occur in these extreme
northern climes, the sky grew heavy with cloud
and snow commenced to fall, smothering the ear-
lier layers, now turned to ice, with yet another
thick carpet. I rued that this snowfall now erased
both our own and the murderers' tracks; these
might have been of assistance in the investigation
into the massacre, which I felt obligated to pur-
sue. Indeed, around the house there were no
tracks visible at all when we left it to return to
the ship. It took us two more nights and two
more days to reach the farthest shore of this
vale of tears. We had to use the oars to make
headway against the wind coming down from the

frozen wastes that blanket the mountains of this country. This wind, loaded with snow, pierced us as with a thousand needles, and the helmsman was able to orient himself only by keeping the shore close to starboard. It was shortly before nightfall that we reached the end of the fjord. I was in no doubt that this must be the very place you had designated in your directions, for, in spite of the snow and the crepuscular light, I could make out the shape of a great church, albeit lacking a bell tower, surrounded by a few houses. A jetty, crudely built of rock and wooden piles, projected into the water amongst large chunks of ice. It had been built to receive ships, but beyond the pier head we saw not a one, neither beached nor anchored; merely some derelict fishing boats pulled up on shore. The place is hemmed in by high peaks, which offer some protection from the wind; I presumed that, despite its forbidding grandeur, animals might be able to survive in such a place and provide sustenance for men.

I debated with the Captain which of three

possible courses was the wiser: whether to make fast downwind of the jetty, the easiest position for unloading our cargo; or to beach ourselves to leeward of shore, as did our ancestors when they came to pillage the monasteries and abduct the nuns to serve them as concubines and domestics; or, last, to tie up at some remove, and wait for daybreak. Notwithstanding the grumbling of the oarsmen and the prolonged suffering which it imposed on us all, it was this third course which prudence counseled me to adopt. Amongst other and important considerations, the massacre we had, if not witnessed, then at least inherited, caused me to contemplate our welcome from my intended flock with caution as much as with hope. I therefore assigned a sentry watch to be posted and ordered that a wall of shields be erected over the gunwales. The season's tardy dawn revealed to us the entire population assembled on the beach, a curiously silent band, gathered around a large cross held aloft by the strongest amongst them. But, whether their paltry boats were too flimsy or too leaky to carry them, or they were worried that they would not be able to regain shore in the stiff gale then blowing, or were simply afraid, they had not attempted, nor were they attempting, to row out and pay us a visit at sea. Your Grace will find this hard to believe, but the water was so cold that to fall in meant certain death; a body would instantly turn into a statue of ice. I shall not chronicle for you the scenes of Christian devotion which ensued. I took the precaution of donning a bishop's stole and capelet ere setting foot on firm soil, so that I would be recognized. One cannot conceive of a more extreme contrast than between this ceremonial garb and the rags which my everyday garments had become: like my companions, I was bundled up in bear and reindeer skins, my legs and feet sheathed in strips and scraps of leather, and had I thought of bringing along a mirror, instrument of better use to the courtesan than to the sailor, I would have seen that I looked more like a wild animal than a minister of God. But stole and capelet, worn over this savage garb, served as my passport, and all of these good peo-

ple welcomed me on their knees; I thanked God
for not giving me the vanity to take upon myself
an homage destined only for Him. These
wretched people, deprived for years of the
Church's succor, groveled on the ice at my feet,
weeping with joy. Never stopping, and with nary
a thought of my hunger, nor of the stinking
breath I was exhaling to the point of being sick-
ened by it myself, I went at once to say Mass in
the church which I already considered mine, as
much to give thanks for having been led here, as
to commend to Heaven the least contemptible of
those souls whose martyred corpses we had so
recently counted. I was glad to find my companions in a similar state of mind: prostrating themselves out of gratitude for their safe passage, and
neither resenting my harshness, which they might
otherwise have construed as cruelty, nor blaming
the Captain for his, they participated with fervor
in the divine devotions ere devoting themselves
to thoughts of food or women. Admirable sense
of priority! What singular obedience to virtue on
the part of these men, more used to the clout of

the whip and the cat-o'-nine-tails than the chalice
and the pall! Even the Captain, whom I always
suspected of placing more faith in observation of
the weather than in observance of ritual, came to
kneel in the church, in the last row with the publicans. In this place there was no need to grovel
for favor: it was simply his way to shew respect to
the man who had had the good fortune to be his
leader, as to express thanks to the navigator who
had guided him hither, and who likewise owed
him the same in return.

My priestly duties gave me leave me to
observe both the place and the congregation. As
for the place, the large basilica, so long ignored by
the Mother Church, had suffered abandonment
of its structures whilst remaining well preserved
in its husbandry. On this last point, Your Grace
will be moved to learn that, in spite of the dearth
of grain, the loaves of unleavened bread had
been prepared for the Consecration. The roof
beams supported the weight of centuries as well
as the weight of the sods that had been added to
it over time; the roof had collapsed in some

places, ruining the masonry. This did not deter me, however, from attempting to assess what massive shipments of wood had had to be ferried hither from the fatherland, across the cruelest of seas, endangering so many vessels and lives, in order to build the frame and the beams. Since there is a lack of good soil or sunlight, and due to the fierceness of the wind, not a single tree grows in the frozen wasteland of New Thule. These lethal voyages were no less than an act of faith, rising like a cry to heaven. The plain windows carved into the back of the chancel had lost their glass, if they had ever had any, replaced here with crudely stitched animal bladders, and there with planks of plain wood. Happily, the light of the divine truth did compensate for the daylight, which was scant at this season, despite the prox-imity to the glacier's glare. In sum, in this church, naught but atrocious poverty, nary an ornament, nor statue, nor treasure: there was but the ancient model of a ship like ours, set like a votive offering in a side chapel, harking back to this impoverished folk's origins in the mists of time, the sight of which gripped my heart. As for the congregation, it did not escape my notice how gaunt many of them were. I will list the causes of their wasting for Your Grace's consideration hereunder; there were many different causes, or they were all one and the same, depending upon one's point of view. Some of these people were disfigured with blemishes similar to those which we had observed on the corpses in the house of the massacre. All wore the haunted air of people on intimate terms with their own death. The whispers of the *Oremus* were only the more fervent for it; the pity their condition inspired in me was offset by the sheer joy of beholding such piety. Their knowledge of the Latin prayers had survived the absence of ecclesiastical oversight, albeit corrupted by the years and pronounced in the accent of common speech. Stirred by the general fervor, I noticed in the back of the church some publicans who were not praying. They seemed different to me from the rest of the people: short of stature but robust of mien, as if their impiety had had two contrary effects: it had

stunted their growth and at the same time rendered them immune to the pestilence.

In olden times the people of New Thule had
no ruler but the Church and the King. But after
being abandoned for so many years by both
Church and King, each fjord anointed a chief,
and while this position was initially an elected
one, it often came to be passed down from father
to son. I pray that this custom will not be construed as rebellion, nor as treason against the
King. It merely harkens back to the practices of
the ancient republic established by the free land-
holders in the days ere New Thule was annexed
to our kingdom, and it would be unjust to berate
these forsaken farmers for the necessity into
which they were cast through our own negli-
gence. Gardar is in Einarsfjord, which, according
to the ancient sages, was allotted to a man named
Einar when the Norsemen arriving from Iceland
settled in New Thule. At least that is what I was
told by Einar Sokkason, whom the inhabitants of

the fjord recognized as their chief — son of Sokki Einarson, himself son of Einar Sokkason, and so forth back through the generations. Thus had the Heavens decreed that I should be welcomed at the very end of the world by a man who goes by the very same name as the one who sent me thither. I was torn between marveling at this coincidence, and fearing that the man might present a threat to my authority. Yet in my heart I did not doubt for a moment that, from Einar to Sokki, Your Grace must be a distant heir to a branch of that same line, albeit one that remained at home.

After Mass, Einar Sokkason led me to my quarters, the one-time bishop's residence, if one might so label the ramshackle hovel that it was. The maintenance of the sole church, which they grandly call the cathedral, had taken up so much of this destitute folk's efforts that they had not the strength, nor the means, nor the hope, to sustain the lodgings of a bishop so long awaited yet ever absent. I shall describe anon, with all applicable relevancies to Your Grace's perusal, the demise of the old priest charged with the cathedral's upkeep for the past half-century since the death of the last prelate, by whom he was ordained.

I disclosed to Einar Sokkason the carnage we had stumbled upon whilst it was yet fresh and the corpses still warm. The house was known to him, but is accessible from Gardar only by sea; it lies at two days' march across the ice, counting the unavoidable detours around crevasses and ravines; the ice is a mass of naturally formed outcroppings, and it is so treacherously weak in places that it can easily swallow up the traveler; for although solid enough to block ships from passing through, it is by no means firm enough to warrant that a man may always safely step on it. There are no boats in Gardar seaworthy enough to retrace our journey to that accursed place. As for attaining it by land, which in happier times was possible once, as he had been told by his father Sokki, Einar informed me that one would have to scale the vast and forbidding frozen plateau which extends over the entire interior of this land, and march some ten leagues ere descending again, encountering a thousand crevasses; and that no one had ever made it back from such an expedition. Many years had passed since any habitant of Gardar had seen anyone from the farm they call the The Vale, at the place called Undir Höfdi, near a long-abandoned church which once belonged to the cathedral's diocese. Einar showed little emotion when he learned of the death of ten of his liegemen. In answer to my queries as to possible motives or culprits, he replied only with indifference, hardened as he was by seeing death all around him, even in his own family, falling on innocent beings who did not deserve their sorry end, which they owed to no other violence than that brought about by nature and the famine.

The crux of my report will diverge somewhat from what Your Grace had envisioned. As far as churches, only the so-called cathedral of Gardar survives. All that is left of its appurtenances is ruins — chapel and outbuildings, belfry, stables, stores, forge and other dependencies, stripped of every last timber, mute testaments to a lost prosperity. The treasure, if such ever exist-ed, vanished so long hence that the people have memory neither of it nor of the cave that may have served as its vault. Moreover, gold is of no use here, other than in the feeding of avarice: for the destitution is so absolute that even the rich-est gold could purchase nothing in exchange. Similarly, all livestock, pastures and fields owned by the church have either been stolen or confis-cated. It is verily a miracle that the faith managed to survive the evaporation of all her material sub-stance. As for any other earthly assets these peo-ple might possess, the task Your Grace assigned me, of taking inventory to assess the tithing, is a simple one. There is, to all intents and purposes, nothing left. To describe the poverty of these wretches is to wish to share it. The winters have become so much more severe since the first set-tlers arrived that only some few dozen acres are still under cultivation on the least exposed ter-rain; yet even there, shelter from the wind must not bring excessive shade, for in summer the path of the sun across the sky is as brief as the sigh of a dying man. The vast river of ice coming down from the northeast, rumbling right up to the settlers' doors, blasts a frigid breath upon the land. The sight of the byres breaks one's heart. For want of a good haying, the udders are withered and the flanks hollow; the cows can no longer calve. Rather than let them die, the people slaughter the cows for their own survival; they devour everything, down to the marrow in the ribs, they suck on the leather and the hooves, they gobble the eyes as if they were eggs. Some households do not burn the manure for heat: instead, they dry it, mix it with chaff and eat it. The sheep, left to fend for themselves without shelter, have not the strength to forage for sustenance beneath the impenetrable ice. Many a father is faced with the grim choice of killing the livestock for survival, thereby sacrificing the entire year's food supply to the hunger of today, or else of starving to death with wife and children whilst watching his herd waste away. It is rumored that some deaths are attended by unspeakable feasting; there may even be a secret covenant which dictates that a cadaver's flesh belongs to the family of the deceased only if that family be comprised of more than six souls; if not, the extra meat is doled out among the neighbors in a monstrous travesty of rationing. For want of wood or iron, once carried hither from Europe on cargo ships but no longer, they do not have the implements necessary for fishing or hunting. The boats take on water, despite being patched with moss and bone-glue, or animal hides lashed around the hull. Such measures cannot overcome the ravages of time; I know of boats which had once belonged to their owners' great-grandsires, still in use despite years of hard service. On account of the ice, driftwood torn from the shores of Markland or Europe no longer washes up on the Settlement's shores, as it did erstwhile. Hence are they cut off from the source of that commodity, so vitally needed to replace the missing lumber shipments from home.

Einar Sokkason gave me the following list of farms and place names, but begged me not to count them in assessing the tithe: since for difficulty of access many of them had been so long cut off, he was not at all sure of their occupancy. The Settlement's southernmost farms are at Herjolfsnes, not far from the Port of Sands where the cargo vessels arriving from Europe once used to anchor. From there the goods would be ferried by rowboat to the most isolated farms situated at the far reach of the fjords. But this traffic had ceased with the advancing ice. They say that all the people there perished from a pestilence brought upon them by some heresy, or from the famine, and that a mass grave was dug for the dead by the dying just before they too expired. It pains one to think that these last survivors, at death's door, had not the time to dig for themselves a proper Christian resting-place. North of Herjolfsnes lies Ketilsfjord, named after its first settler, Ketil, a comrade of Erik, the founder of the Settlement. Not a soul lives at Ketilsfjord today, which is all the more deplorable because in ancestral times the church of the Holy Cross prospered there in the place called Aros; it owned everything in the vicinity, fields, pastures, peat bogs, stream and river beds and banks, lakes and their fish, cliffs and their fowl, islands, islets and reefs, together with their shipwrecks, so valuable for their timbers and the booty in the holds; when I demanded that he confess that they might have engaged in the abhorrent practice of luring ships onto the rocks, Einar replied that he would never have risked sacrificing riches destined for the common good to the profit of but a few. I shall leave it to Your Grace to weigh the sincerity of such protestations. On the larboard banks of Ketilsfjord, just before its endmost point, a monastery of the order of St. Olaf and St. Augustine had been built in a secluded spot at the foot of some fearsome and colossal mountains, with lands equivalent in size to those of the church at Aros: so that between these two ecclesiastical domains there was nary a freeholder from whom even a nominal tithe could be wrung in exchange for his soul's salvation. But according to what Einar had gathered, it would matter not a whit how this region was apportioned in the end, for it would be an apportionment of naught, since all were dead in Ketilsfjord from its mouth to its farthest reach.

North of Ketilsfjord comes Alptafjord, which had been settled only by some very inferior and isolated farms, about which none, not even the wisest elders, could recall anything remarkable. North of Alptafjord comes Siglufjord, which is or once was wholly owned by Benedictine nuns. The fate of these women lies shrouded in mystery. In answer to my questions, I received from Einar but a strained silence, which might well lead both Your Grace and myself to the most alarming suppositions. I cannot imagine that without men to help them with the tilling and the husbandry, nuns could survive the ever-intensifying rigors of nature. I asked myself with some concern why, if that were so, Einar refused to speak of it, and, if it were not, why he would not tell me what he had gleaned from the reports or sagas. Even further north lies

Hrafnsfjord, with two farms which have not been heard from since the ice closed in, and after Hrafnsfjord comes Einarsfjord, the place whither we were directed by You, by God, and by our own navigational skills; here there are twenty-four farms whose condition, depending on the sun and wind exposure, the impact of the ice on sea and land, and the health of the inhabitants, runs from the most abject misery to the most grueling poverty. Here is a list of the men to whom these farms belong:

On the right bank, south of Einarsfjord, Egil Egilsson, Gudmund Skallagrimsson, Thorvald Björnsson, Solvi Hafgrimsson, Bjarni Sigurdsson, Snorri Thordarson, Jon Hakonarson; on the left bank north of Einarsfjord, Arnlaug Stefansson, Leif Herjolfsson whose family long ago came from Herjolfsnes, Steingrim Olafsson, Tyrkir the Teuton, who, it is said, is a descendant of one of Erik's companions, and thus has no more German about him than his surname, Jakob Krakason, Johannes Ulfsson; at the top of the fjord and around Gardar, Einar Sokkason, Thorir known as Man-of-the-East, great-great-grandnephew of serfs who worked at Petursvik for the Benedictines of Siglufjord, Harald Ragnarson, Thorfinn Arnaldsson, Arne Arnarson, Sigurd Njålsson whose ancestor of the same name had a great reputation as a mariner in these parts, Stein-Thor the Pagan who does not believe in anything yet ceaselessly protests the contrary, Hermund Kodransson, and Simon Magnusson.

These twenty-two farms or homesteads house three hundred and twenty-seven souls, some more devout than others, but Einar had no doubt that they would all take comfort in my presence.

And further north still lies the Settlement's largest fjord, Eriksfjord, still accessible on foot or even on horseback: in summer it is a two-day march along the shore over hilly terrain, with several very perilous river fords and glaciers to cross. Two summers have passed since anyone from Eriksfjord last came here, or vice versa. It counts ten farms which are the property of the descendants (real or professed) of Erik, the man who first settled there in the dark night-ages; so that their pagan or Christian names — Erik, Tryggve, Knut, Helgi, Brand, Fridrek, Olaf, Rasmus, Per, Solvi, Poul — are followed by the surname claiming that lineage: Eriksson. All of these farms are located in what was once Erik's domain at Brattahlid. To assess their condition and population, it will be necessary to journey thither and interrogate their chief, for no doubt these people have anointed one; but that was all that Einar knew of it.

Legend has it that at a great remove north of Isafjord there once existed another settlement, of which there has been no news for more than a century. Some claim that the settlers there have abandoned the faith and the Christian virtues; others say that they have all perished, and one wonders if that is not the preferred outcome. It makes my heart bleed to think that this leaves but a choice of two possibilities, death or heathenism. Even farther north, at a distance greater yet, at the very pinnacle of the world, lie the glacial solitudes where, legend has it, our forefathers' forefathers betook themselves to hunt all manner of wild beasts. This was before the ice came to gird the land nigh perpetually, and they were still able to reach it by boat. They would bring back bear and musk ox meat, salted and cured on the spot, snow hare and blubber-fowl preserved in ice or in whale-oil, and, for trading, bear, fox and other animal furs; also leather and tusks of the sea-unicorn and the sea-lion, happy substitute which, with pious deception, might pass for ivory. Thus did the poor, at negligible cost, feed their families in catering to the appetites of the rich, whilst at the same time supplying the church with precious artifacts. From Greipar and from Krogsfjord they brought back the most precious commodity of all: drift-wood. Floating tree trunks and branches torn from the new territories, Helluland, Markland and Vinland — places the people would mention with the hushed reverence due to a paradise lost and gone forever — were swept north at the mercy of tides and wind. Upon the availability of such wood, more precious than the jewels of

Palmyra, depended this wretched people's ability to build the ships which averted the need to wait for the vessels from Europe, as for some messiah that never comes, enabling them instead to venture thither themselves to sell their pelts and their false ivories, and return home laden with vital commodities for their settlements. But those times, as I have said, are long past.

Einar Sokkason did present to me the one surviving priest; although it must be said that it would take an uncommon combination of mettle and faith to persist, upon the sole strength of his erstwhile ordination, in bestowing the august title of priest on the porcine monster which he cast before my feet. I thanked Heaven that this wretch was no longer in a fit state to celebrate the Holy Sacrament, which would certainly have been a sacrilege in light of his depravity. Crawling with lice, his mouth oozing a foamy phlegm which gave off a rank smell, and holding by the hand a scarce-pubescent female publican, he spewed a hundred blasphemies which could not be ascribed to inebriation, since they have no strong water in this forsaken part of the world. The obscenity of his relationship with that young witch made a perversion of every word he spoke. Fornication, to him, was a thing to gloat about, at the very moment when his blasphemy aimed at absolving it. The abominable details, which I cannot bring myself to record here, rendered even more odious the age difference between himself and the child whom he had the temerity to call wife; of the two, it was hard to know which had perverted the other, since nature should have brought back to the old man the innocence which is not yet lost in youth. I at once determined to send them both to the stake, he for heresy, apostasy, sacrilege and sodomy; and she for venery worked through sorcery. It occurred to me that the benefit of this twofold punishment would itself prove twofold: first in asserting my authority, in being seen to use immediate severity, thereby saving the need for still greater severity later on; and second, in imposing on the guilty pair the punishment which their sins so amply deserved.

I ordered them to be burned at the stake the very next day. One obstacle presented itself to my plan, namely the lack of firewood; I said hay and straw should be used, to which Einar responded that they had not enough hay to feed the livestock and that the famine would grow more acute if it were used for that purpose, no matter how negligible the quantity consumed. We agreed, therefore, to employ a mixture of peat and seal-oil to burn the accused, a wise economy, since it preserved the animals' fodder whilst drawing out the sinners' agony, a meet result for a proper atonement. However, when the time came to light the pyre, the publicans gathered in loud protest and I had to call for protection from my sailors. To the pleas of the womenfolk, aggrieved at the fate of one their own, and one of the youngest to boot, I responded that in sentencing them to the stake I shewed compassion and kindness, since had we followed the custom of our forefathers, such an execrable sin would

have called for the procedure known as the
bowed trees, in which two trees were bent low to
the ground and the victims hung from their feet
at the junction; the trees then being abruptly
released by slashing the cords that had tied them
down, so that the victims' bodies were cleft in
two like a carcase of beef. I explained to these
poor women that, stirred by pity, I did not wish
to be judged overly harsh, nor be accused of fail-
ing to take into account the constraints of our
times. Also there were no trees to carry out that
manner of execution; but I thought it best not to
discourse on that matter.

It took me a while to understand what these
publicans were, for none spoke of it openly; in
reading this Your Grace will no doubt have
found the answer ere I did, though I went among
them every day. So does the Holy Spirit see fit to
parcel out wisdom. If their station was not that
of slaves, their condition certainly was. They
were bastards and the descendants of bastards

whom our Norsemen, with their dissolute habits, had engendered on the women and maidens of the gnomes they called *skraelingar*. At the time of the great ice age, these *skraelingar* had settled at the mouths of the fjords, where the infernal viands they like to eat are found. They had arrived in small numbers, and with the savage stealth of their kind. Over the years there have been encounters, massacres, and some trade, including of the womenfolk, whom these natives will gladly sell in exchange for weapons or hunting implements. So it was that our Christians committed the folly of trading the safeguard of their future salvation (since such practical items as weapons cannot be replaced) for the fleeting joys of debauchery. I was told that these women were very apt for carnal pleasures, both submissive and gentle, but that they withered as quickly as mountain blooms, so that the transports of the flesh must presently cede to the charge of their keep, made more burdensome still by the general poverty. Moreover, our Christians were wont to enslave the seed of such unions, thus receiving recompense for their keep, and, I shudder to relate it here, to draw into their beds the outcast issue of their own fornications: so it seems that on this point Your Grace's instructions did indeed contain a just premonition. These publicans are Christians only in name. Oppressed by the very families to whom they are bound by blood, reduced to the most menial labor and the enslavement of coerced concubinage, they have cast from their hearts the Church teachings of their masters' faltering faith. So it is that their very existence continues and exacerbates the vices which gave them life. In deliberating with Einar and my men, I considered exterminating the lot of them. However, not only did I see but little of Christian nature in such an enterprise, I presently came to realize that it would harm some of the settlers' interests as well. Only the poorest, the sickest and the feeblest among them were without possessing such publicans. If it so happened that these most destitute of Christians, through their illicit couplings, managed to produce any such bastards (an unlikely event since the publican women were shrewd enough to prefer fornicating with those more favored by destiny), the offspring would usually leave the homestead of their birth to offer their services where there was greater prosperity. But I further perceived that the publicans exercised another, more subtle, hold over the Christians. I was told that their tribe, on the whole, appeared to be immune to the scrofulous, pestilential and parenchymatous sickness which was ravaging the Christian population; so that, in spite of their natural indolence, these publicans still possess sufficient energy to go hunting or fishing at the margin of the ice; as for husbandry and such agriculture as the climate allows, they are incapable of it, their ancestors never having had the inclination for it, nor the opportunity. So, I am told, in those households where they are numerous, the publicans have increasingly turned providers, and in some cases, in an abominable reversal, the slaves lord it over their lords, who, stayed from killing them for fear of want, do not even dare to whip them, had they the strength to do so.

The rigor of winter gave way to a brief summer respite, which brought the populace some relief since the livestock could be put out to pasture. My companions and I rejoiced to find fresh water in liquid state again, which made it possible to bathe, something we had not been able to do since casting off from Kirkesund the previous year. I was filled with awe at the way in which God compensated for the gloom just past with a sudden profusion of flowers. Some publican hand illuminated my hovel with bouquets of flowers which were regularly renewed. Around the solstice, and in spite of the proximity of the mountains to our south, I was even fortunate enough to witness some sunshine lighting up saxifrages and potentillas, which the Saxons and the French call *quintefeuilles*. But the weather's cheer was o'ershadowed by grave and troubling matters.

The execution of the unworthy priest and his publican whore did, certainly, have a dampening effect on the practice of slavery, but not on fornication, nor incest. I was aggrieved to discover that, in one of those reversals whose cause

is known only to the Evil One, it was now the
Christian women who seemed to be giving themselves to the publicans, including their own sons
and blood relatives, in order to assure themselves
of nourishment and keep; for the vigor of these
men, and their skill at hunting, had now made of
them more desirable mates than the Christian
husbands enfeebled by illness and starvation. I
came to consider this a sin of minor consequence
compared with the calamity of the women's criminal apostasy. For the publicans whom they chose
as mates in return for food, eschewing such religious teachings as they might have received, and
in spite of my presence in the cathedral, were
returning to the evil arts of their ancestors, who
worshipped only things of nature, such as the
wind, the ice, the streams and the animals of the
wild, which, in their ignorance or perversity, they
endowed with a spirit and either a vengeful or a
benevolent will. Their Christian concubines
became tainted with this heresy. My men and I
surprised more than one of them in the travesty
of mixing Christian prayer with barbaric rites on

hallowed church grounds. Even the language was corrupted, a mishmash of Latin and our native tongue, with a smattering of the unintelligible gibberish spoken by these hunters. I urged Einar Sokkason to call a clansmen's council, promising him that my men, armed for the occasion, would keep the publicans at bay. Einar lauded my great resolve in the struggle against heresy, evoking with admiration the just torture of the old priest and his concubine; he deplored the rise of paganism and the women's indecent conduct with the publicans. "Can you not see," he cried, "that not only do these harlots welcome them into their beds, living with them in a state of prostitution, as it were, in which their caresses are paid for with a few strips of seal meat; do you not see, also, that the women have become so attached to these publicans that they are willing to abandon their own hearths to live with them the life of savages? Mark their teeth, and cast out from you those women whose teeth are worn down from chewing leather. That is sinful work, it sullies the mouth that is intended to receive Our Lord.

Mark their smell, and banish those that reek of fish or ammonia, for that is a sign that they have adopted the publicans' habit of washing their hair in urine. Repudiate your wives and disown your daughters if you catch them indulging in pagan rituals. Let them die rather than succumb to these ways!" Then it was my turn to speak. "You must persecute the heresy which has infil-trated the Faith. You must no longer tolerate the rites taking place in the back of the cathedral while I am dispensing the benison of the Mass — these tambours, these walrus-ivory drumsticks, these dances of the caged bear which too often accompany the hymns which I have taught you. Denounce those publicans who have the effron-tery to pose as preachers; I will have them burnt at the stake. You will know them by the multi-tude of their gods, you who have but one, by their belief that there is a great soul in the moon and that the dead are reincarnated in those who are named after them. Never confuse incantation with prayer." Einar, in a transport of passion, then betrayed my leniency and the prudence of my policy by calling for a massacre. I disputed to the best of my ability the legality of such a vote. It was not up to the people, I said, to override the authority of the Church on matters of practice and creed; that task was mine. Some of the elders defied my authority by arguing, against all reason, that this was a civil conflict. Were the publicans not stealing their womenfolk? At the very least, were they not serfs, upstart farmhands suspect of rebellion? A great many of them, moreover, were the illegitimate seed of their clan, and it was the right of their sires to exercise freely their ultimate authority over them, as custom would have it. Much as I tried to argue, on this last point, that the Gospel does not confer on the father a life-or-death right over his children, they came back at me with the Bible and the story of Abraham; I had not thought these peasant minds capable of drumming up such learned argument. The assembly ended in confusion and bloodthirsty cries; it spilled out along the shore, around the houses, in search of victims. I was forced to send my men out after them; so now,

instead of guarding the council from the publicans, they were suddenly obliged to defend the
publicans from the council. Sadly, it was not
God's will that no blood be spilled that day. So
did three of the most prominent Christians lose
their lives, but not before killing an equal number of publicans. Thus did I find myself waging
war on my own flock. Some of the women, with
tears of supplication, staggered toward me along
the beach and clasped me by the knees. The
blood from their wounds seeped crimson into
the melting snow. I warned them that even
though I had taken upon myself to be their pro-
tector, they ought not to toy with Your Grace's
envoy. I had one of them whipped, and she died,
although that had not been my intention. Sadly, I
was unable to prevent her corpse from being
thrown to the dogs. However, this unhappy
incident did, fortunately, manifest my judicial
evenhandedness toward Christian and publican
alike, and it proved to them that I would not
shrink from punishing either side's trespasses.
My impartiality was evident from the blood that

was spilled equally by both camps. Then the rampage died down, quenched by this policy, and no less by the satiation that the appetite for murder finds in its accomplishment. Einar Sokkason and the elders went down on bended knee before me and begged forgiveness.

This was not the end of my troubles, nor of the civil unrest. I spent the solstice attempting to quicken in my flock the flame which was so prone to being extinguished. With the help of two young publican maiden, whose heads I ordered shaved as a sign of their humility, I set up a hospice in the back of the cathedral for those who were most severely ill. So did the area which had once been usurped for sacrilegious dancing and fraudulent pagan worship become a resting place for dying Christians. I ordered food for them to be confiscated from the granaries and fields to ease their last moments on earth; let them die, if they must, but not of starvation. For my men and I were well cognizant, from our own experience, what sort of foretaste of hell such a death might be. I must credit Einar Sokkason for his humanity and also the brute force with which he assisted me (overcoming his initial reluctance) in stifling the settlers' recriminations. It was a folly, some said, to give the dying the precious food so vital to the survival of the living! To which we replied that they who were alive today were the dying of tomorrow. They also objected to the use to which the cathedral's narthex was being put, in stead of its intended design; I reminded them that Jesus favored the sick over the hale, and that His house was the antechamber to Heaven. Better to have the faithful lying prone in the back of the church than to have the irreverent on their feet in the chancel! Finally, they argued that the publican women sullied the cathedral by their presence; I invited the Christian ladies to come and tend to the dying themselves. None responded; thus by their silence did they answer their own objections.

I now turned my attention to reclaiming the land for agriculture, throwing myself and my companions into the effort. In these climes, hay-making is of the utmost urgency, for only hay can lend the livestock, perforce the humans, a chance of surviving the winter. Assisted by the Captain, I mustered the ablest of the men. The Captain, accustomed to taking command, roused the sleepers and the bed-ridden, sent our sailors out to the isolated farms, rallied his crew by cajoling or putting the fear of God into them, and put them to work singing the songs of their home-land. It was a miracle to see these cadavers return to life in order to ensure a food supply which would be of little avail to most of them. It was a marvel to hear the sea shanties sung over the hay bales, conjoining our homeland's two greatest treasures, her land and her sea. Nor did the Captain confine himself to rounding up the Christians to work. All publicans not employed in the fields were sent out on hunting and fishing expeditions. The fish were dried in the sun, and the seal meat hung to ripen in the shade, as was the custom of their race. Forceful persuasion was needed to convince the publicans to kill more than their immediate appetite, for when they have filled their bellies, albeit for the nonce, they become slothful, and fritter away in games and idle chatter the precious time the short summer allows to make ready for a lengthy winter. Moreover, since they, or at least the least savage among them, were aware that such provisions were disproportionally earmarked for the Christians, their flagging zeal made it necessary to goad them on with the strictest threats once they had assured themselves of sufficient food for the next day or two.

The Captain pressed into service even the children, whom he organized into gangs to go and catch birds with nets, and to gather their eggs from cracks in the cliff face. The eggs were kept for winter either by being preserved in ash, or left to age until they rotted inside the bodies of seals gutted of their entrails, depending on whether they were to appeal to wholesome

Christian appetites or to the corrupt palate of the publicans, who are disposed to delay the eating if the deferral enhances the flavor. Some of these children were so weak that they were unable to cling to the cliff face with their feeble fingers; they would crash onto the beach or the ice below, where they were promptly devoured by wolves. But the regrettable loss of these young lives was overshadowed by a scourge of greater cruelty, that of the mosquitoes. The Captain, my men and myself were astonished at how fierce these were, outdoing even the mosquitoes in our country, accustomed as our people are to these pests since time immemorial. Anyone who has not experienced the start of what only the devil would maliciously dub the "best season" in these remote parts has not yet set foot in the maw of hell. The insects we have at home are as naught compared to the billowing, all-obscuring clouds of mosquitoes which blight New Thule and swoop down on her denizens with insatiable greed. Nor do they spare the animals, which grow maddened by them. These attacks last until the end of the month of August and are followed, I was informed, by an increase in the pestilence, which, coinciding with the return of winter, often strikes the very people who were theretofore spared. Thus the tolerable relief of the sun comes wedged between the evil of the mosquitoes and the scourge of the maladies following close upon the insects' disappearance. Einar and I frequently discussed these plagues, which had arrived quietly, making their first appearance just a few years before my arrival; whereas the mosquitoes had been there since the beginning of time. Therefore to blame these insects for the pestilence was to pass summary judgment without due process of law. The population of Gardar and the surrounding fjords had ever been prey to the maladies that are common to humankind the world over, albeit here further aggravated by the brutal cold. New Thule was ever a place where reigned the curved spine, the stiff back, the crippled haunch or knee swollen with the humor, even more than in our fatherland, where such afflictions are nevertheless so prevalent that none thinks of complaining of them. I blamed these tribulations upon the set-tlers' uneasy relationship with God, and on the icy conditions in which they were compelled to live. Yet, somehow, they had been spared the agony of leprosy. The pestilence, however, was a different matter. The publicans being largely exempt naturally rendered them suspect, although they were never blamed for it; I lauded Einar for not succumbing to the temptation of attributing the ills of nature to sorcery, and for having taken pains to prevent such suspicions from whetting a thirst for vengeance when it came to the settlers' quarrels with the publicans. He responded that there were sufficient bona fide grounds for complaint against the publicans, not to have to resort to questionable ones. From this I saw that were it not for respect for my authority, Einar would still be nursing the same hatreds for the publicans as did his fellow citi-zens. The publicans' immunity to the disease made it unlikely that exhalations of the miasma or the swamp-land vapors were to blame; an improbable likelihood in any case in such an icy country, since those conditions afflicted both races equally. As for the mosquitoes, although I deemed there to be as much reason for doubt as for assumption, I ordered as a precautionary measure that the houses be fumigated and the exposed parts of the body slathered with bear or seal grease. None of this did any good, however; for either the mosquitoes thrived on such deterrents, or else the people failed to observe them. The torments did not cease and the pestilence grew more severe. It was then that one Jörgen Ulfsson Jorsalafari, the Jerusalem Farer, came to my attention. His surname told the story: that, not content with journeying to Mauritania in quest of riches, he had later voyaged to the Holy Land in quest of salvation. There he had acquired the art of spinning yarns, adopting the ways of the Orient. He told such outlandish tales that only a man who has traveled as extensively as I would give them credence. As a trader he had purchased elephant ivories, priceless compared to the tusks of the walrus or narwhal, and lion skins far more suitable than New Thule's bearskins for adorning a knight's harness or draping a rich merchant's bed; he had collected, he said, a flock of luscious blue-cheeked concubines who accompanied him everywhere, and whose sensuality, made all the more alluring by their silent reserve, helped him to endure the sweltering nights. I knew from my sojourns in Italy and Spain that across the seas there exist races whose black skin disposes them to both servitude and concupiscence. Had I entertained any doubt as to the veracity of his tales, the accounts of the Roman gentlemen, or of the Count of Ascoigne, would have rendered them plausible. But it was above all the light which he involuntarily shone on the massacre in the vale that lent them credence. He told me that he had brought with him from the orient a little monkey, which he had come to love like a son, and which followed him wherever he went. He had not the heart to part with it when upon returning home he set out for Iceland, with the intent of purchasing wool to be sold to Continental merchants, defrauding the tariffs of the Hanseatic League. From Iceland, a storm out of the east had swept him all the way to New Thule, where his vessel, laden with wool, had foundered in Einarsfjord. There he was plucked from the water by a coastal farmer, who had sheltered him for ten months. The monkey had through some miracle survived the perils of the voyage and the rigors of the climate. When the moment came to depart in order to seek elsewhere the possibility of a voyage home, Jörgen Ulfsson, having lost his gold, his wool and his companions in the shipwreck, found himself at a loss to repay the farmer for his hospitality. The farmer's children loudly clamored for the monkey in payment; they adored it, nor could Jörgen have refused them, since the animal would not have survived the lengthy march over the ice to Gardar.

All sorts of rumors sprang up about this monkey, a species of animal heretofore never encountered by these simple folks, and baleful legends grew up around it, holding it to be a Beast of the Revelation, and blaming it for the pestilence, which had indeed first broken out at that time.

Chapter 3

HE CAPTAIN SET OUT AT THE END OF
JUNE. It had been decided, in consultation with
the Bishop and Einar Sokkason, to mount an
expedition north to find out if there were any
other settlements there, and to hunt game in
order to flesh out the winter provisions. The
expedition turned out badly. The Captain
steered The Short Serpent in a northerly direction, hugging New Thule's west coast. He was
hoping to put in at the Western Settlement,
which according to legend was situated a dozen
sea leagues (four hundred miles) north-west of

Gardar, and which, the same tradition claimed, had last been heard from in Gardar "three generations past," without giving further detail. The Captain was bound for the hunting grounds to the north, vaguely referred to in local parlance as the "Land of No Houses", two-weeks' journey by sea from Gardar. So the Captain had estimated that the round trip would take a month, with another fortnight thrown in for hunting, plus a fortnight for disembarkation at the port of call and for exploring the Western Settlement and its environs, with the option of cutting short their sojourn if need be. By these calculations, they would be home at the end of August. The Captain had taken pains to find out what kind of traveling speed this estimate of days at sea and distance covered was based upon; albeit that they had no direct experience of it themselves, the elders had been able to glean some useful information from their ancestors' accounts. So the estimate was based on the number of days on open sea within sight of land, in fair weather, not counting any hindrance or detour occa-

sioned by the ice, with, they said, smiling, contrary winds but every other day. Since *The Short
Serpent*, like all the ancient ships upon which she
was modeled, was capable of making headway
against the wind even though her rigging consisted of a single square sail, of sailing close-hauled,
and of making progress, thanks to her sturdy
oarsmen, even when there was not a breath of
wind, the Captain estimated that their average
speed, taking into account all contingencies,
would be one-twelfth of a sea-league per hour
(approximately two and three-quarter knots). A
month, then, for a return voyage of sixty marine
leagues (two thousand miles), discounting ports
of call, or thirty leagues (one thousand miles) to
reach the Land of No Houses. What transpired
showed that the Captain was too optimistic. At
the Western Settlement, which *The Short
Serpent* reached within the predicted week without difficulty, the Captain and his comrades
found nothing but devastation. Around the
ruins of a large church they came upon abandoned farm buildings with caved-in turf roofs

and crumbling walls. The stables and gardens were littered with the remains of sheep, cows and horses. Scattered human skeletons, still in ragged scraps of clothing, were testament to a sudden and violent end, with no opportunity for a decent burial. The sailors combed the houses and the outbuildings, although they were aware even before they set out that since so much time had gone by, there was little hope that they would discover any soul yet alive. They found nothing worth taking back with them, and it was in vain that they explored the surrounding land. The most isolated farms, remotely situated in hills or valleys, were likewise deserted. The Captain, who had taken care to bring ink and vellum, drew a map and some rough sketches to serve as his report. The Short Serpent left the area on July 15th, heading north-west along the shore. They did not reach the Land of No Houses and its extensive hunting grounds until a fortnight later, fifteen days of battling a strong head wind out of the west-northwest, with squalls, rain, snow and poor visibility greatly increasing the danger of collisions with icebergs. Here they stayed for three weeks, trying to fill the barrels and chests with their game and catch, which turned out to be rather meager, although fortunately there was enough sunshine on the south-facing slopes for the meat and fish to be dried. Bears rarely came along on the floating ice; but the one-year goslings, prevented by their molting plumage from taking wing before the winter migration, were abundant prey, easy to catch and to conserve in their own fat. The men of The Short Serpent made a great slaughter of them. They also killed some seal and walrus, although these men of the Continent found the meat revolting. The Captain kept a vigilant eye on the white glitter of the sea, heralding, several miles north of there, the ever-approaching ice. Then ice crystals began to form along the coast, congealing into sheets of ice at night. The auks and the fulmars abandoned the steep cliffs towering above the sea, which were bleached white with their droppings. These were signs that unforgiving winter was at hand; it overtook The Short

Serpent and her crew sooner than expected. The Captain promptly initiated the necessary preparations with such haste that it surprised his crew. Men were dispatched to fetch the chunks of meat left on the hillsides to dry. Salt was scraped from the stagnant pools of seawater in the fjord's ends for pickling the last catch. The birds, once they had been thoroughly cooked in their own fat over peat and bulrush fires, were packed into the barrels. The men, who could think of nothing but that they might go hungry, were loath to renounce their hunting and fishing in order to ready The Short Serpent for the return voyage. The Captain had to assert his authority, and to point out to them how dangerously the distance between the sun and the horizon had already shrunk. As they left, their oars had to crack a skin of ice until they were half a mile offshore. At the mouth of the fjord, the Captain spied the ice slowly approaching from the northern horizon.

For three days the ice left them an open channel of a dozen miles or so. Wending their way south along this channel, they covered some

two hundred miles, having to use all their inge-
nuity to dodge the icebergs. The Captain, who
favored truth over diplomacy, did not attempt
to conceal from his men that, notwithstanding
this favorable run, there was yet a distance fourfold greater to traverse before they would reach
their point of departure. As the temperature
dropped, the ice began to fill in behind them,
and presently it was all around them. The
Captain found a torturously meandering channel of open water close to shore, but it was a
respite of short duration. Every night brought
an atrocious freeze. Mindful of their experience
on the voyage out from Kirkesund, they warded
off the cold as best they could with seal-oil-burn-
ing lamps, lit under the shelter of the poop
deck's tarpaulins, which had congealed into a
ceiling of ice. The helmsman had to be relieved
every two hours, lest he freeze to death. The
Short Serpent finally became trapped in the ice
on the day of St Ingrid (the 2nd of September),
having gone four hundred miles since leaving
the Land of No Houses. They were still six hun-

dred miles from their destination, by about 72°
north latitude.

Nightfall. Two men were bickering on the
ice.

"Where did you see the great umiak?"

"We were hunting seal, at the hole in the ice,"
said the younger one.

"Where did you see the great umiak?"

There was never a direct response, for fear of
appearing boastful and upsetting the Spirits.

"It was almost all day ere we killed a seal,"
said the younger one.

"Umiak, umiak!"

And again: "Umiak! Umiak!"

The question became an insistent refrain,
then the subject of verbal sparring.

"Umiak! Umiak! Young turd," said the older
one. "Will you tell us where you saw the umiak,
yes or no?"

"Umiak! Umiak! Old turd," said the young
hunter, "the great umiak! the great one!"

By "umiak" they did not mean the traditional women's boat, which would never have turned up out there, lost on the vast ice sheet. The great umiak, that was something else. The young hunter had mentioned it in passing and then refused to surrender any further details, to annoy his elders. The dogs growled and yelped in their sleep, their noses tucked under their tails.

"Why don't the elders try to guess?"

The exchange of insults — "old turd, young turd"— continued until well into the night. The young hunter finally gave in, pointing in a certain direction, which they would commit to memory by noting the lay of the rippled snow on the ice, at right angles to the prevailing wind. The great umiak lay at half a night's march. This information provoked a flurry of excitement and activity. The men unloaded their sleds and hid the seal carcasses beneath blocks of ice. They set about untangling the dogs' traces, using their bare hands and teeth; it was an excruciating job in such extreme weather. The sleds set off slowly by moonlight over the jagged crust of the ice sheet. The men trotted alongside, cracking their whips. When the young hunter estimated that they were drawing close to the spot where they would be within earshot of the great umiak, they stopped to regroup. Silently the men chewed on their wads of frozen seal blubber. Some urinated on the ice, holding the dogs at bay with their whips for fear of exciting in them an excessive interest in the strong stench emanating from their crotches. In the warmth of the winter huts, in the glow of the oil lamps, there was often much jeering at the poor bastards who, having neglected this precaution, had been mutilated by the dogs and become the women's laughing-stock. The verbal sparring that was their princi-pal distraction focused in this case on the dog's tongue, which, according to the chanted jibes they liked to exchange, would replace the sex of the maimed men. "Tongue! Tongue! You use your tongue to lick instead of going inside!" said one. And another: "Dog's teeth! Dog's teeth! Your wife's belly bites and snaps shut instead of lapping it up!" The women would laugh, baring teeth worn down from chewing on animal hides.

But at this particular juncture the men did not laugh, and the talk was entirely focused on the action. Roles were assigned, just as on a bear hunt. The oldest man would stay with the dogs, whose respect for his whip was manifest in the scars it had left on their noses, ears and tails. He was to stop them from devouring the leather harness and the food. "Young Turd" would show them the way, which he would find in the moonlight by noting the orientation of the ripples of the snow, and by following the tracks. They dealt out the harpoons and bows and arrows before slipping off into the night.

As soon as the Captain opened his eyes upon awakening, he was startled to see light coming in beneath The Short Serpent's overturned hull. Sunbeams glancing off the horizon were finding their way inside the shelter through the crack between the gunwale and the surface on which the overturned boat rested. With their experience of the previous year still fresh in their minds, the crew had taken the precaution of closing off that gap with casks, bundles, crates of food and blocks of ice, all packed under the tarpaulins that were laced around the hull like a skirt by ropes threaded through holes in the ice. Now both provisions and tarpaulins were gone; the gunwales rested on the ice blocks alone.

The Captain lost no time counting his men, and slipped outside. Three mutilated bodies lay there in pools of frozen blood. Arms, legs and heads had been hacked off, apparently with an axe. The Captain roused the survivors, fifteen in all, and, when they had digested the sheer horror of it, they conferred what to do next. Four men, including the Captain, would set off in search of game. They would take the hunting weapons and some skins to serve as a tent. The dozen men remaining, including the boatswain, would stay under the shelter of the overturned boat and await the return of their comrades. The Captain shrugged off the question of what these men would do for food, if they could not leave the boat to hunt for themselves, unless it should land in their laps by some extraordinary stroke of good luck. Their assailants, for fear of over-loading themselves, or perhaps scared off by the stirring of one of the sleeping men, had left one casket of seal oil behind, and this would have to suffice to keep the lamps lit so that they would not freeze to death.

The Captain opened up for debate which direction the hunting party should take. Ulf Jonsson declared he was for the traditional way. Scoring a cross into the ice, he said they should sing a counting ditty (Saint Paul! Saint Olaf! Saint John!) to determine which branch of the cross pointed in the direction where they were most likely to find game. That was the way they used to do it in winter, in his native valley, before setting out to hunt the snow hare. The others seconded this idea. But the Captain calmly argued that a counting song was no substitute for plain reasoning.

"But I've drawn a cross. God will decide."

"God is not interested in deciding where we should hunt," said the Captain. "He grants us the freedom to decide these things for ourselves."

"Don't you believe that God takes an interest in whether we live or die?" demanded Ulf.

"Of course I do," said the Captain.

"Well then! If we foul this up, we're dead. So it's up to God to tell us which way to go."

The sailors grunted their agreement. The Captain, a man of action rather than of faith, pressed for the common sense option. It was to the south that the animals fled the approach of winter. It was in the south that they would find the ice thin enough to cut the holes required for catching seals. It was southward that the tracks of the looters led. It might be imprudent to go after them in quest of revenge, but at least they could follow them from a distance, since the attackers had gone in that direction to hunt. They should therefore go south. The men, exchanging glances, finally agreed. Then the

Captain called upon the unnamable. Notwithstanding his indifference toward God when it came to the practical decision of which direction to follow, he now called on Him to come to their aid. Did not God desire the faithful to come through this alive, lost as they were on the ice, and preyed upon by heathens more savage than wild animals? The heathens had stolen all the food his men had taken such pains to collect. But they had also left behind three mutilated corpses. The Captain saw this as a providential sign. He made the following calculation for his crew: twelve men, including the boatswain, were to remain behind beneath the shelter of the overturned hull while the remaining four would go off on a hunting expedition. These four, who would be in need of sustenance until they managed to find fresh game, would take with them one of the victims' remains, which, preserved by the cold, they would tow after them on frozen skins serving as cargo sleds. They would thus leave behind two of the dead; the Captain estimated the weight of these at two hundred and fifty pounds. For twelve sheltered and inactive men, with an oil lamp to keep them from freezing, there was enough there, based on one pound per person per day, to hold out for over two weeks, deducting leftovers of one-fifth which hunger, if prolonged beyond two weeks, would eventually force them to eat. Without betraying this grim doubt, the Captain thought it unlikely that all of them would survive that long. Death, in taking some of them, would increase the others' rations; the survivors would eat the dead if the need arose. The Captain laid out this plan with an infectious calm. Just one man began to weep, and Ulf Jonsson turned around to vomit. Both were mocked by their comrades, who upbraided them for forgetting that Christ himself had offered up his body as a sacrifice; and that he had done so even while yet alive, when his blood ran still warm in his veins. The boatswain, who had already assumed command of his little band, decided that the flesh would be eaten frozen, for he determined that the disgust would be lessened if it were uncooked, and did not give off any smell. Upon hearing this, the Captain judged the boatswain to be up to the task, and felt he could safely leave him in charge of the crew.

The Captain and his three comrades set off towards the south. Ulf Jonsson soon proved to have been a bad choice for this expedition of last resort. He never stopped complaining and lagged behind continually. This surprised the Captain, because, although not an exceptional seaman, Ulf had been quite up to the job aboard The Short Serpent, where his endurance at the oarlocks was much appreciated by his peers. It was this physical strength of his that had made the Captain pick him for the hunting party; but events were to prove that he lacked the necessary moral fibre. For three days they marched without food. The Captain guessed that they had covered less than twenty miles, but kept this estimation to himself lest it discourage his men. Eager to set a faster pace, he led the way, hoping that shame or fear would impel them to follow him by example. He never turned around, and refused to stop and wait for them until nightfall. So the others realized that unless they kept up with him, losing sight of their leader would mean losing their way, and their lives. Their progress over the ice was agony. Boulders of ice, crevasses, icy scree and snowdrifts made every step of the way a back-breaking ordeal, rendered more excruciating still by the prospect of being indefinitely repeated. As they marched south, the blinding sun, glancing off the ice, scorched their frozen faces, which were soon just a mass of raw flesh crusted with oozing sores. They resisted smearing their faces with the seal oil, for they had to save it for keeping themselves warm at night beneath the hides that were their makeshift tent. Added to these tribulations came the snow-blindness. The interior of their lids began to itch intolerably, and the sun's rays bored into their eyes like red-hot needles. The Captain set the example of walking with his head down instead of keeping his eyes on the horizon, and of knotting a blindfold torn from his tunic over his eyes, with two narrow slits to see through. That way the light was less cruel, but the eyelids remained inflamed and sore; soon they began weeping pus.

On the morning of the fourth day, their pace ever slackening, hunger finally drove them to eat the human flesh. They tore off frozen gobbets of meat using the tips of their arrows, taking care at first not to pierce the entrails, which aroused in them the greatest revulsion. This squeamishness would presently pass as their hunger grew, except in the case of Ulf Jonsson, who obstinately refused to eat and who grew horribly nauseated at the mere sight of the human meat. He lay down on the ice and declared that he would go no farther, not even to save his soul. His comrades, unable to convince him to get up again, called out to the Captain for help. The latter retraced his steps, stopped when he reached Ulf Jonsson and, seizing him bodily, swore to him that they were at no more than two days' march from open water and seals to kill. Ulf pleaded with him: could they not cut a hole in the ice right here to catch some fish? He would eat the fish raw, as long as it was frozen. The Captain explained to him that the ice here was too thick, that they would die in the attempt to break all the way through the ice shelf, even in the improbable event that they just happened to be standing right above a school of fish. Ulf Jonsson knelt down on the ice and, weeping, began digging at it with his bare hands. Soon his fingers were nothing but bloody stumps. The Captain then threatened to kill Ulf on the spot, rather than allow him to delay them and demoralize the entire team.

"And," he said, "we will eat your corpse if hunger compels us to it." This threat gave Ulf just enough mettle to continue until nightfall. But he could not fall asleep and kept his comrades awake with his incessant groaning. Soon contempt and hatred replaced the sympathy these rough men had at first felt for Ulf, and the Captain, who was half awake, had to lie down beside him to protect him from them. For although he was prepared to sacrifice Ulf if necessary to save the rest of the company, he had no desire to see his mission corrupted by base murder. The makeshift tent let in an intense cold, despite the seal-oil lamp, and they had nothing but the clothes on their backs to serve them as bedding. They arose the next morning spent from shivering all through the night, all encased in a shell of frozen sweat. Both Ulf's state of mind and his behavior grew worse. He walked so slowly, halting so often, that in less than an hour his comrades had gained half a mile on him. Then he would plop down on a snow bank, and beg them to come back for him. More than once he stretched out on one of the frozen pelts they were using as sleds, and demanded that they pull him. The others kicked him off, and would have finished him off then and there had it not been for the Captain's intervention. They killed a fulmar, abandoned by its migrating flock; they had been watching it for several hours as it circled them in hope of food. The Captain, who had stayed close to his men in order to prevent a brawl over how they would split these modest spoils, offered the bird, still warm, to Ulf Jonsson, turning a deaf ear to the other men's protestations. Ulf tried to drink its blood, but promptly vomited it up again. He said that he would eat only the liver. The Captain tore out the liver and handed it to Ulf, who stuck it into his mouth, kept it there a few seconds without managing to chew it, then spat it out again, gagging. One of the other two men caught it and wolfed it down greedily. That was when the Captain made the decision to sacrifice Ulf for the sake of the expedition. Ulf lay down on the ice as his comrades moved off, screaming after them at the top of his lungs, until they were out of earshot. Then the Captain went back, kneeled at Ulf's side and asked him if it were true that he would not at any cost go any farther. When Ulf replied in the affirmative, the Captain knocked him unconscious with a block of ice and then stabbed him through the heart with a knife. Next he said the prayer for those who perish at sea, and they resumed their march southward.

Night fell. The Captain, alone, two miles ahead of his men, stepped onto some fresh ice, and it foundered beneath him. He managed to swim back to the edge, smashing the thin layers in his way until he found ice thick and solid enough to support his weight. As he tried to hoist himself back onto the surface, he thought he would die of sheer exhaustion. The rags which served him as gloves had instantly frozen solid, hampering his movements as he tried to catch hold of the icy outcroppings. In order to hoist himself aloft, he had to pound his hands on the surface to smash the ice that had stiffened the gloves, but he felt his strength ebbing in the water, and his fingers were too numb to hold on much longer. He did, however, manage to grasp hold of his knife — the same one he had used to kill Ulf. He jabbed it into the ice, which was level with his nose. Now, clamping the hilt between his palms and kicking frantically with his legs, he was finally able to haul himself up onto his stomach. To his horror, he found himself on a little island cut off from the main ice pack by a channel that was growing ever wider, bearing him away from his companions and from the shelter they would erect for the night and which, with its oil-lamp, was his only hope of survival. The islet,

blown by the wind, was moving south; the channel was turning into a narrow ocean inlet. Even
though it was dark, the Captain could tell he was
moving, from seeing icebergs sail by. He made a
tour of his sanctuary, which measured no more
than a few hundred square feet, so that when he
got near the edge his weight caused it to tip into
the sea. Thus he could not even, in a futile effort
he had briefly considered, use his bow as a sort of
rudder to steer his floating island. Hunger and
cold soon drove out his fear. He heard a seal
sputtering, but decided not to shoot blindly into
the dark, lest he waste one of the few precious
arrows in the small quiver slung across his chest.
Besides, even if he had hit it and killed it on the
first attempt, how would he have hauled it up
onto the floe? There was nothing for it but to wait
calmly for death, sitting in the middle of the
islet, which would keep colliding with other
blocks of drift-ice until, gradually, it was eroded
away to nothing. Behind him, his companions
would soon reach open water, where they would
be able to hunt quarry and catch fish. When they

had obtained sufficient provisions, would they still have the strength to return to the shelter where the rest of the crew was waiting for them? The Captain considered his own fate with serene detachment, troubled only by his worry for his men. While thinking such thoughts, he suddenly felt the breeze die down. Snow began to fall. The Captain built himself a shelter of ice blocks, lay down inside it and fell asleep. He awoke to a brilliant day filtering in through the blocks, but these had now been soldered together by the frozen snow, and the Captain found himself imprisoned in a narrow coffin. He tried first to kick the bottom out, but with no space to draw back, his feet lacked sufficient force. He noticed, too, that he had no sensation in his feet, and realized that they were frozen. Wiggling around, inch by inch he managed to grasp his precious knife, which was tied to his right thigh by a leather thong. The effort, which took him an hour, melted the layer of frozen sweat which had coated his body under his clothes like a carapace. Taking the knife in his right hand, he chipped at the mass of ice and frozen snow pinning down his left arm, which he finally succeeded in freeing. Now he was able to switch the knife to his left hand, and began trying to dig out the wall behind his head, but in vain. His left arm was weak; he thought his right would be stronger. So he took the knife in his left hand and used it to free his right arm in the same manner in which he had freed his left arm with his right hand. He was drenched in sweat by this time; and then his hunger returned with a vengeance, hampering his efforts. From the light filtering in he could tell that it was already past midday by the time he was able to set to work on the wall behind his head with his right hand, which now held the knife. He had to keep sweeping to the foot of his shelter the ice shavings his knife had scraped off, or risk being blinded or suffocated.

It was not until the following night that he was able to see the sky above his head by rolling his eyes back . But the struggle to free his shoulders and extricate himself from his ice-tomb still lasted all night long, and it was already light

out, in the late-dawning morning, when he finally took his first tottering steps in the snow. A
happy surprise awaited him: at the whim of
winds and tides, his little island had drifted
back toward the main ice-sheet and was joined
fast to it! He had not eaten in two days. He now
commenced to walk north, to find his companions. Clambering laboriously up onto a hum-
mock or a névé, he would scan the horizon in
every direction, worried that he might pass right
by his companions without seeing them, since he
did not know the exact trajectory his island had
taken as it drifted north and then back towards
the ice pack. His feet, frozen numb, did not cause
him any pain, but the lack of sensation made
walking difficult. He fell down into a deep
swoon, and awoke to find himself lying under a
makeshift tent erected by his two companions
after they happened to stumble upon him.
Eagerly he bolted down the morsels of human
flesh they offered him, but mindful of the risks of
overeating after a lengthy fast, he was able to
curb his hunger. The worst thing still needed

to be done. Gangrene had set in on one of the Captain's frozen feet. Swollen to enormous proportions, the size of man's head, it gave off a revolting smell. Because they had not wanted to weigh themselves down, they had not brought an axe. So the Captain commanded one of his men, the lightest one, to place his knife across the foot where it met the toes, wedging the tip of the blade into the ground by putting all his weight on it. He ordered the other man to jump onto the hilt with both feet. Blood spurted from the amputated toes. The Captain, who had been given pieces of leather to clench between his teeth, uttered scarcely a groan, nor did he pray to God.

This method, he claimed, was less cruel than the one the publicans had introduced to the New Thule Settlement, which consisted of having rats trapped in a wicker cage nibble at the rotten flesh of the ailing limb.

Chapter 4

W

WHILST AWAITING THE RETURN OF THE Captain with a desperation that did test the limits of my faith, I issued some mandates in the name of Your Grace, with the intent of improving and reforming the settlers' habits, which had been corrupted by their suffering and by consorting with the publicans.

First I considered the poverty of their garments, or, rather, of their rags, because even the least poorly dressed among them was garbed in naught but tatters. The wasting of the flocks meant a dearth of wool; the few sheep which did survive, thanks to the diligence of half-frozen shepherds, had scarce any wool; and the art of weaving had been lost and supplanted by the craft of the publican females, clever at tanning the hides of marine creatures using the teeth and saliva. Heaven disposed, as did the light of Grace which surely Your Eminence shone on them ere e'en I was dispatched to convey it thither, that these pagan furs be reserved solely for the heretics who made them; our good Christians would rather perish of the cold shrouded in the wool of our Savior Lamb (albeit in such short supply), than allow their wasted bodies to be defiled by these hides but half rid of their rancid fat. Moreover, the publicans themselves were no longer in any position to trap these beasts of the apocalypse, having long since abandoned the shores where they are to be found. In light of the above, I found it even more contrary to divine law and common sense that these people should hew to the outlandish fashion of the long trailing hood, thereby wasting on vanity and ornament wool that would serve a far more practical and decent purpose if it were used to ward off the cold and wind. It is a curious thing, is it not, this absurd need for frippery and excess when the basic needs are not met? In this craving Your Grace will detect, no doubt, the work of the Evil One. His seductive powers tempt the people to forget the true necessities, not least that of salvation, in exchange for the vices of frivolity, such as dress and physical adornment. Do we not see the savages of the Orient, the very negroes of Africa, even when they are reduced to eating grasshoppers, yet piercing their lips with coral, and studding their teeth with pearls? Or their women, whose breasts hang like empty winesacks, unable to suckle their children, yet who stretch out their necks with stacks of copper necklaces? Ah, miserable creatures, to forget that in order not to offend God, ornament, vanity and extravagance are to be reserved solely for the rich man! For the sumptuousness of his finery deprives him not of the bare necessities; he knows how to allocate his spending in the sparing proportions which allow for the satisfaction of all his needs. Only he whose table is abundant has the license to adorn himself. Such is not the case with my most wretched flock. This fashion, mainly for the ladies — a relic from our ancestors abandoned long ago (save in some remote Icelandic valleys), at the time when St. Reverian resigned from the service of the Gonzaga princes — was first conceived as a way to tuck the hair inside a low-hanging cowl at the neck. The thing spread to the humble peasant wives, and then to their husbands and their sons, so that eventually no serf worth his salt would be seen in a hood trailing a tail less than a foot and a half long. As for our Norsemen of Thule, the poorer they grew, the further they took it; so that today, as I write these words, the children have three feet of wool hanging down their backs, the men and women four, hampering their movements and whipping through the air or water whenever they nod their heads. One cannot help but feel pity for the pus-oozing eyes and gaunt cheeks peeking out from such extravagant headgear, as if the wretches were seeking thus to make good their sufferings. Therefore, in God's honor, I banned any hoods hanging more than six inches below the back; I had any that were longer snipped off. I cleared a work space in the cathedral so that the young maidens, under the sage supervision of an older virgin (or at least one who claimed to be such) might be put to work unraveling the excess wool, and use it to weave and sew new tunics and capes. My maids were quick to learn the art of their ancestors, and produced some lovely articles of clothing which I distributed to the most needy, although some advocated that we sell them for profit instead. But for what currency could we have sold them? For sheep, perhaps, now all skin and bones, whose scant wool was insufficient to produce similar items? Or for some pieces of gold dating from the time when there was still trade with the fatherland, but which since the trading had ceased were no longer of any use to anyone?

Objections were raised to this sumptuary regulation by the vainest among them; others attempted to avoid it by hiding the forbidden accessory under their hair. I had them all whipped.

Second, I was determined to protect the children from their parents' cruelty, a common enough consequence of sordid poverty. In this undertaking I was supported by our creed: Your Grace's lessons have given me an understanding of the barbarity bred, if I may say so, by extreme privation, which drives people to sacrifice a son in order to save the father, or to save the mother by killing the daughter. What kind of hope is there for Your Grace's teachings, or for the lessons of the Gospel, if the young die before their elders, if the daughter is destined to perish ere she has emulated her mother in the sacred task of giving birth, thereby subverting the God-given order? A nice thing it would be if the holy saints, and the doctors who have discoursed so learnedly upon these topics, were ere long to be heard nowhere but in the graveyard! I therefore prohibited the exposure of infants, which was such a common

practice in the poorest households. It was a custom they had adopted from the publicans at their
barbaric worst. Whereas in our society the abandoned child still has a chance of survival if God
wills it, whether it is surreptitiously deposited at
the Judas-hole of a nunnery's tender-hearted
portress, or left under a sheltering portico, or
tucked into a box lined with dry straw and moss,
my poor flock had adopted from the publicans the
practice of leaving the naked child exposed on the
ice, or even lying under some stones, stacked up in
such a way that the purported shelter becomes
both the instrument of its death and its tomb.
This is done to ensure that no passerby will find
the baby and rescue it, only to reunite it with the
very folk who wanted to be rid of it in the first
place so that they should have one less mouth to
feed. Some make a great pretense of concern,
going so far as to stuff a piece of seal lard in the
infant's mouth, which is supposed to prove to anyone who might happen along and unearth it, that
its parents did not mean for it to die. I determined that, in extreme circumstances, it would

have to be other way around: the parents must starve to death for the sake of their children, leaving them the scant nourishment made available by their own sacrifice. I even went so far as to permit, nay, what am I saying, to *sanction* children, driven to the very brink, to send parents or grandparents whom age had rendered utterly useless into a final exile in the frozen wastes of the High Country, whence no one has ever returned. It was not without torments of conscience that I did resign myself thus to violate the most solemn of Your Grace's commandments. The fact that I was, as it were, encouraging patricide, albeit compelled thereto through mortal necessity, did not accord with the respect I owed to the fourfold paternity which engendered me: my flesh-and-blood father, humble tool of the three loftier paternities: God our Father; Your Grace, without whom I would be nothing; and finally Our Most Sainted Father in Rome, thanks to whose good offices I am in some small way the thing you are. I beg Your Grace to bear in mind that I was but emulating the sacrifice which Our Supreme Father made for

His children, Who went so far as to offer up His own flesh for our sustenance. Hunger has its own wisdom, and the cold its own charity. It was the Devil's will, with consent of the Eternal One, that I follow the publicans' example in these matters. In fact, it is their wont to persuade the old to leave home as soon as the infirmity of age renders them useless for hunting or fishing, when they are no longer capable of hurling a harpoon or of rowing their peculiar oars, and to betake themselves to the High Country's icy wastes. They are banished with deference and also with sternness, as befits both the natural ties of the blood and the aged ones' utter uselessness. These poor wretches depart without a word, without a farewell, without regret, to expose themselves of their own free will to the wolves, or to the cold which will bring them eternal rest. So it was that a distinctly pagan custom became my Christian flock's saving grace. I even had to rein in their zeal somewhat, for I caught some of the most famished ones chasing away their parents by pelting them with stones, after blinding them so that they would not find

their way back. I pray to God and beseech Your
Grace that this barbarism, which grew out of
their overstepping rather than obeying my actual
orders, will not come back to haunt the people of
New Thule.

Third, I rid the Settlement of the execrable
travesty of simulated strangulation, a practice
popular with the children. Let me make it perfect-
ly clear to Your Grace: this was not a game in
which the poor tykes played at sending an imagi-
nary murderer, thief or sodomite to the gallows,
chasing and catching him, and finally delivering
him to one pretending to be the hangman. Such
play would have been pure innocence, and the
children might have gleaned some useful lesson
from it for the edification of their souls, for it
would have taught them that crime is always punished, even if the game should happen to result—
by accident perhaps, or in the heat of some cruel
prank—in an actual death. The children of

Gardar, however, indulged in quite a different sort of perversity. From their confessions, and from an embarrassed Einar Sokkason, who informed me of it, I gleaned that they would hang themselves, or have their playmates strangulate them, in order to feel, through the obliteration of consciousness, the giddy sensation of hovering on the verge of death, which they did claim to find thrilling. Since most of them did not believe in heaven, or had no concept of it, it was not the threshold of Paradise, certainly, which sent them into raptures; it was the obstruction of the humors flowing into the brain which caused them to experience transports of giddiness, similar to the effect of a strong ale, or else of those intoxi-cant leaves, pungent yet pleasant to chew, which some of the Crusaders brought back from the Orient.

I had two reasons to condemn this practice as heresy: first, for the danger it posed to the life of these children, either through some mad desire to prolong the strangulation, or perhaps through the carelessness of the friend who was supposed to end it by releasing the rope; but even more for its aim of cheating death in attaining a bodily paradise, in substituting intoxication for virtue, and in allowing an instant of folly to replace the deeds of a lifetime. Finding a suitable punishment for such an outrageous offence was not easy. I had misgivings about having the sinners put to death, since it would have been an odd sort of retribution to grant the criminal the very thing which he sought in committing the crime; besides which, I was reluctant to kill any children, even with just cause, particularly since, between the hunger and cold, they did not, alas, need my intervention to die. I did consider the amputation of one of their limbs. A foot was out of the question, however, as was a hand, even the left one, since that would only have meant imposing the care of more crippled youngsters on the villagers, when the labor of the least feeble among them was so crucial to the survival of all. I finally determined that the guilty should have one eye gouged out, a penalty harsh enough to discourage them from trying it again, whilst preserving the abilities they would need (with the exception, perhaps, of archery) for hunting, fishing, herding or plowing.

Fourth, I vowed to stamp out the manner in which our little populace settled its disputes and administered that which in other climes might be termed justice. It seemed to me that their form of jurisprudence was something they had perniciously adopted from the publicans, whom I saw holding secret tribunals, sometimes in a corner of the cathedral, even during the sacraments which I had reinstated, or screened by a wall of turf. Our Norsemen, driven by hunger and cold to become slaves to their own slaves, who were better adapted to the rigors of the climate, were drawn in little by little, adding a touch of Christianity to the proceedings. The decline of the Church, and, in spite of Einar Sokkason's alleged sway over the farmers of the region, the absence of all civil authority, had left the field clear for the heretical practices which I feel bound to describe to Your Grace. But where else could they have turned? What inquisition (absent pyre or stake) was there for them to appeal to, what sovereign (absent a royal guard) was there for them to bring their disputes to? What recourse did they have, beyond settling their quarrels in blood if they were angry enough, since there no longer was any gold or silver coin to allow them to impose a monetary fine to compensate a wrong? Before an assembled people's court, they would open the proceedings with some guileless ditty, similar to a children's song or adapted from ancient publican legends, where Your Grace will note that their profane bestiary was tricked up with a saint or two, so that it was flavored with a dash of the sacred. So, for instance, ere delving into the details of some cuckoldry (one of the most common types of disputes, in spite of the cold, which one would think ought to have tempered the passions), I heard the two parties go at each other as follows, one in the guise of an eagle, the other as a codfish, in an exchange repudiated by Nature:

THE EAGLE: I have a lovely mustache
                   And a fine ear

THE CODFISH: Saint Reverian, hear my
                   cause,
                   Sitting on a rock,
                   Sitting on a rock.

THE EAGLE: Saint Plectrude, plead my
                   cause,
                   Sitting on a rock,
                   Sitting on a rock.

THE CODFISH: May Saint Reverian cut off
                   your mustache
                   And stopper your fine ear,
                   Sitting on a rock,
                   Sitting on a rock.

How these simple souls, deprived of the splendor of Your Grace's light, as well as that of Your august predecessor, had managed to keep alive the memory of Saint Reverian and Saint Plectrude, both dear to my heart but not commonly cited in Christian prayer, is something which I shall leave to Your Grace to determine. Despite the confused understanding made manifest by such a mishmash, and the barbaric sacrilege which tainted the remainder of the procedure, I was touched by these faint traces of devotion, which had found their way here, through the ages, from the abominably deep and dark forests of France.

But this, if I might say so, was no more than a foretaste of their justice. Soon the two opponents, on their feet in the center of the circle, commenced to take turns at improvising a long chain of bitter barbs, to the beat of the tambour. Nothing escaped the sourness of their mockery: neither their adversary's looks, not a single blemish of which escaped insolent commentary; nor his smell, often quite pungent (albeit that the publicans had little to envy one another on that score, whilst their stench was surpassed a hundredfold by our Norsemen, whose misery led them to neglect the body's cleanliness); nor the worst qualities of the soul or character; nor even the misfortunes brought about by the whims of destiny. Then the plaintiffs' wives would commence a tirade against their husbands, thereby taking the opponent's side, seeking to settle a score about some sexual frustration, or about unwelcome caresses, or beatings, or having been unceremoniously traded to a neighbor. As for the smell: *Analurshe, Analurshe,* which means "old turd" in the publicans' tongue. On a toothless mouth: "You like to suck because you cannot bite," with its lewd double meaning, accompanied by roars of laughter, which Your Grace will discover under such rude remarks. On the unspeakable sexual congress with animals: "Don't mix your milk with that of a cow", or alternatively, "Don't put your prick in the mare's ass; if she gets to her feet, you'll be left dangling". The hunter who came home empty-handed, the fisherman who caught no fish, were publicly crucified in the same manner: their children were summoned and mockingly served a mush of peat soaked in seawater. These innocents would then spit in their fathers' faces for being such poor providers. The loser in this war of words faced a cruel punishment. He whom the crowd, by its jeers and jibes, judged to have lost the contest, had no recourse but to betake himself into permanent exile. For this was the custom they had adopted from the publicans: that not a friend, parent, child, nor neighbor was henceforth allowed to talk to the loser, nor help him in any way, so that he was pitilessly banished. Not only had the unhappy man lost all honor and respect, which, to a people so cut off from the world, is more vital than blood is to life; he had lost everything else as well — home, freehold, fields, cattle, children, slaves and wife. This was all the more painful when the instrument of his betrayal had been his own kith and kin. The only thing left for the banished was the white immensity of the High Country. Thus did end in death what had begun in song.

As when considering other criminal aberrations, I was greatly torn in deciding on a fit punishment to eradicate this one: for how to impose an appropriate penalty, that is to say death, on a practice which itself leads to death? Would I not be making myself an accessory to the very crime I was supposed to condemn? Taking refuge in prayer, I received guidance from the Holy Ghost, and Your Grace's proxy, in the form of a happy expedient. My verdict, then, was to have the winner put to death instead. I did have some brief concern that the people would be astute enough to consider the ruse of deliberately losing so that they might eventually come out of it the winner, since their adversary was to be punished by death; I foiled that gambit, however, by sending to the stake one or two who did try to win by losing. The result was that the incentive for these disputes promptly dried up: for who would want to win only to lose? From that moment on, my justice, that is to say, God's justice, was the only one to hold sway over the foothills of the High Country.

Finally, I banned the horse fights. Seeing starving peasants indulge in such a pastime, as futile as it is costly, seemed to me the antithesis of piety. These men should have been spending in meditation upon their imminent death whatever leisure was left for their vices after battling the withering away of nature and doing such farm chores as the cold would still allow. Some sought to excuse the indulgence by citing the horses' increasing uselessness, as the ice advanced upon lands which had once been arable. But I would not accept their argument: if the horses were indeed no longer of use for work, then let them be fattened first with hay, however scantily, and then eaten, taking care to spare a stallion or two to inseminate a few mares. Instead of which, from Palm Sunday and every Sunday thereafter until Saint-Luke's day, these emaciated stallions were herded into a cramped enclosure, where, in order to goad them into fighting, they were exposed to the sight of an aroused mare's hindquarters. I am told that upon a time when there was still trade with the outside world, they would make a poultice of bear grease and ginger root, brought here at great expense from the ends of the earth, to be applied, for greater arousal, to those parts of the mare which one could scarcely call private, since they were bent on making thereof the most obscene exhibition. A pair of stallions was then made to stand face to face in the ring before a crowd which whipped them up into further frenzy with its cries and jeers. Each animal's master would prod his steed with a stick fitted with a sharp stone head like the ones the publicans employ for hunting. Great quantities of the poor animal's blood were shed, not only by the owner's cudgel-blows, but also, to be sure, from being bitten and kicked by its antagonist. On certain Sundays, at eventide, I have seen the eviscerated carcases of stallions that had been kicked to death, lying steaming in the icy glacier's breath, while children played in the warm entrails or fashioned necklaces therewith. I finally resolved to put a stop to it when, during one such fight, I saw one of the stallions' owners beating the horse opposed to his own when he saw his horse's courage flagging: Your Grace will understand that such a cowardly act flies in the face of both honor and the rules, be they ever so barbarous, of such tournaments. To my horror, I then saw the horse fight degenerate into a battle of men. The horses' masters began hitting each other with sticks, then with lances, and finally with axes, until the spectators too took sides, bent on annihilating the enemy faction. I thought of the Emperor Justinian and the famous rebellion which broke out during the horse races, when he thought he would lose his throne, and I was emboldened at the thought of the Empress Theodora, who, having started life as a prostitute and bearwardess ere donning the basilical crown, became the saint who saved an empire. Equipped only with my pastoral cross, without the armed support which my crew would have lent me had they not been lost in the icy wastes of the North, I plunged into the crowd, begging them to slay me rather than each other. Einar Sokkason, less sensible to the inspiration of Theodora than I, sought refuge in a stable; I was alone, one against all; but, despite the danger, the memory of the inflexible empress gave me the fortitude to restore the peace. Einar

Sokkason was reluctantly convinced that we should ban the horse fights, armed with the strength of our faith, and with the feeble support of what passed for a constabulary. Thus was happily abolished this deplorable custom, inherited (I am told) from our distant ancestors.

The next morning, as I was sleeping off the aches of these troubles, a young boy who served me both as sacristan and attendant awakened me to inform me that The Short Serpent had just been sighted on the fjord's horizon. When I arrived, the ship was being hailed with tears of joy by the villagers already mustered on the beach as, driven by the oars, she pierced the mists swirling above the seas where ice, and God's peace, held sway.

The sailors' eyes and their bodies betrayed traces of unimaginable suffering, surpassed only by the horrors of Our Lord's Passion. Three of the men had been massacred and dismembered by unknown brigands, who had stolen all the game

and the fish-catch they had gathered from the
Land of No Homes. The crew had partaken of
human flesh, even on fish days , whilst a small
band marched south under the command of the
Captain in search of open water and quarry,
yet not without losing one doughty oarsman. I
observed that one of the Captain's feet was
wrapped in a sleeve of sorts, made of leather, rags
and rope, and bristling with icicles of frozen
blood. He told me that he had had to have it
amputated because of its rank smell, and I never
found out more about it, for he was not a man
to seek pity. The team that was sent south had
finally attained the edge of the ice, after the singular fate of marching toward a continually
receding destination, and had brought back an
abundance of seal fat to the other crew members
left behind in the shelter of the overturned ship
just as, having run out of cadavers to eat, they
were about to starve to death. The sublime
courage these men subsequently displayed
should be enough to move Your Grace's entrails,
albeit that, according to the Captain command-

ing them, religious piety played but scant part in their salvation. They sawed the boat into as many sections as necessary to allow them to haul it across the ice. For this strange transport they used sealskins, hardened and polished with their own frozen urine. After many days of being harnessed like animals to these makeshift sledges, using their feces for the runners, dragging their disassembled ship across the ocean of ice and subsisting on naught but seal fat, they finally reached open water. There they lashed the pieces of the ship together again with ties, pegs, mortise and tenon, like the shipwrights of old, and set off in the hull thus refitted. But the south wind was strong and contrary enough to slow their progress to such an extent that they were compelled to toil at the oars day and night, battling the ocean's wrath all the way until they reached the mouth of Einarsfjord, where by the grace of God they found a warm welcome from us in what had become their home port.

At the time of these events, a young publican maid dressed in rags was brought before me; she had just arrived from the icy wastes of the High Country. I was told that she had approached the village on her knees, seeming to pay no heed to the sharp grit of these shores, pleading and wailing to be pardoned for sins which she had not committed. Here was a manifestation of religious zeal quite unprecedented for a maiden of her race. Her tale was one of suffering and death, no less horrific than the agonies which the Captain and his crew had suffered both on the ice shelf and on the ocean. I encountered some difficulty sorting out the tangle of her story, and had to turn to Einar Sokkason for help. The remembered atrocity had created the most harrowing confusion in the girl's mind, and it was well nigh impossible to understand the gibberish in which she spoke, impure mixture of the ancient tongue of our forefathers and the satanic patois of the publicans. In order to sort it all out somewhat, and stirred by pity, I strove to spread over her the gentle mantle of divine mercy. I ordered that she be given a piece of barley bread, albeit a sparing portion, aware of the danger of sudden satiety after a long famine. She moaned with pleasure as she took into her mouth the crumbs of barley which I held out to her like the host, for, sweet and gentle soul, she chose to remain on her knees in my presence. She slipped back into the publicans' language so frequently that I had to send for an interpreter. I was given a little gnome, yellow and insolent, whose attention was immediately seized by the blue stain around the poor maid's mouth. "You have killed your brothers for food," the gnome said to her, and, upon my faith, it seemed that these simple folks held that a port-wine stain around the lips was a sign of such an atrocity. Your Grace will forgive me for assuming that there was no more to this accusation than the most naïve superstition. But from her muddled speech, and the interpreter's inadequate services, Einar and I thought we understood that she had indeed killed two little brothers whom she had taken with her into the terrors of the High Country, fleeing the greater terror of something which no Christian would call family, nor home, in any human language. If she were to be believed, and I believed her without hesitation, it was not a matter of crime, but of charity— when the mea-ger provisions had run out which in preparing for their flight their older sister had slipped inside in a sort of pouch formed by the lining of her tunic, these unhappy children had been on the verge of starvation, and complained of it so bitterly that she had hanged them to put them out of their misery. I saw no crime committed here, nothing which called for retribution from Your Grace or from God. I asked her to tell us what she had been fleeing at the risk of three lives. I do not have the heart to repeat it to Your Grace, for it is impossi-ble to do so in terms inoffensive to the ear. Suffice it to say that this maid was born at the convent at Siglufjord, ten days' march from Gardar over the High Country, issue of the coerced union of a Benedictine nun with one of the gnomes that had little by little insinuated themselves into the serv-ice of the convent. Of this convent, of which I have already given account to Your Grace, naught remained, neither altar, nor relics, nor treasure, nor attendant priest, its crumbled walls rising no higher than a man's head, and good only for shoring up the ignoble shacks which the fish-stinking hunters of the eider or web-footed bird had the temerity to call houses, and which they abandoned as soon as autumn was nigh. I did catch a flash of understanding in Einar's eyes, which revealed to me that there had long been wind of this ghastly affair, and that he had been careful to keep it from me. The nuns of St. Benedict, of blessed memory, deprived of pastoral authority and besieged by the intensifying cold, let their herds die out and their farms perish when they forsook the plow, the scythe, and the hay. The gnomes in their service, skilled at catching the web-footed bird and the bear, whose fat one can eat for want of aught else in case of famine, and also the abominable seal, in those places where the ice is broken up, became their lovers, their husbands and their masters; lovers if one can apply that word to people who rut like animals, husbands if one may so call pagans who recognize as holy nuptials only an abduction promptly attended by the crudest of copulations: for that is how their tribe marries and procreates, producing children which multiply like pebbles ere they perish of the cold; masters because the nuns, lured by the promise of food, were then reduced to the rank of slaves and treated in a way that our serfs would not even treat their animals. The fornication is done in public, by lamplight, in full view of the children, and well nigh naked, making no distinction between the right side and the wrong. The women are shared in a free-for-all; these people will exchange their daughter or sister, if she be nubile, for a bearskin, or if she is under age, for a rabbit skin, or if she is past the age of menses, for a walrus tooth, thereby rendering legitimate, commendable even, the most monstrous debaucheries, and all the most unnatural. They worship the male member the way we worship God, they flaunt it under indecent undergarments of fur and encase it reverently in codpieces of musk-oxen bone, and the fellatio to which they constrain the women is their own diabolical version of the Holy Communion. They will gladly lend their wife to any passing stranger in return for borrowing his, to accompany them on a hunting party if their own wife be pregnant or indisposed, or is too occupied with sewing or tanning. Though the husband may lend out his wife if he so fancies, this does not prevent the greatest violence if the woman should freely give herself to a man not her husband; it is considered acceptable then for the husband to kill his wife in cold blood, just as if he were strangling a sled dog considered too slow for the team. When the omens presage a great catastrophe, or the odious charlatan who passes for their priest warns that there is one at hand, they will trade the women amongst themselves, in order, they say, to mislead the evil spirits, who will be deceived by the embarrassment of too many harbors available to their lechery in a village thus transformed into a brothel. The newborn girls are killed off so that their mothers' milk will dry up, for it is the wont of their race to suckle their young for long duration, which would prevent the mothers from conceiving again promptly in hopes of a boy. The dread of this eventuality was what our young publican female, brushed with a tinge of Christianity, told us had made her flee; she herself was carrying in her womb the fruit of such a barbaric mating. On Candlemass she was delivered of a stillborn daughter. Thus did her flight nevertheless result in the very outcome which it had been meant to forestall.

Chapter 5

INCE I WAS SCHOOLED BY YOUR GRACE
EVER to be a friend to informers, those zealous
helpmeets of divine justice, I heard out more than
one person who came to tell me about Jörgen
Ulfsson Jorsalafari, the man who had come from
the Orient with a monkey. I was told that he dab-
bled in evil spells and indulged in invocations and
sorcery; it was even bruited that the monkey,
whose talents and charms he readily trumpeted,
was none other than his own son. It was said that
he had sired it by copulating with a goat, that ani-

mal of easy virtue, as alien to my flock as any monkey, and considered equally vile. A mystic who
came to me as an informant swore to me on the life
of his mother (she was rather long in the tooth, to
be sure), that the monkey had thirty-six teeth in its
mouth and six fingers on its left hand, and that
therefore it carried the sign of the Beast according
to the Revelation at Patmos. He claimed that St.
John, on his island parched by a sun of an intensity
never experienced in Thule, had first calculated
the square root of thirty-six teeth, in order to
extract (if I may be forgiven for the pun) twice the
number 6; that he had then added to it the number
of fingers on the left hand; that in so doing he had
been able to arrive at the Number of the Beast, a
thing which would not have failed to amaze me had
I accorded this piece of nonsense the least bit of
credence. But there is no human folly that does not
contain a grain of truth, nor did the mystic's fail to
do so. I gave him to understand that his knowledge
of the diabolical gave me ample motive to hand him
over to the secular branch, and that a peat fire,
with its special torment of drawn-out agony,

besides providing the villagers with some warmth
in this season of increased cold, might toast his feet
a little hotter than he would like. However, I
advised the mystic, with all the gentleness and seri-
ousness Your Grace had taught me, that I might
not sentence him to the stake if he would do me
the favor of telling me more about the circumstances surrounding the animal's death, as well as
the massacre at the farm of the Vales, in the place
called Undir Höfdi, which is situated not far from
an abandoned church; a massacre, Your Grace will
recall, into whose still-steaming wake we had stumbled when, landing upon the shores of New Thule
for the first time, we had made fast there and
explored the doomed farm. That affair had left me
with a poignant sorrow, in that the first Christians
I had encountered in my mission, at Your Grace's
behest, were naught but savagely dilacerated phan-
toms. I pressed the mystic to divulge if it had been
publicans who had committed the crime. I sensed
that he was torn between the desire to show himself off to advantage and the impulse to confess to
his ignorance; he accused the publicans with such

lukewarm conviction, and such a distorted sense of the consequences of so grave an accusation, that I was inclined to believe they were innocent. I deemed that the hatred which the publicans and Norsemen bore each other, caused by the slave-like state of the former and the latter's own sense of helpless inferiority, was proof enough of the mystic's insincerity, though his blue eyes and blond hair marked him as being of the purest ancestral blood. I employed both blandishments and threats, promising him first the delights of Heaven, then the torments of fire both temporal and eternal, so that he finally gave in and agreed to give me the name of a witness. The witness was Einar Sokkason.

Chapter 6

Ⅴ

YOUR GRACE CAN IMAGINE THE SOLEM-
NITY OF Einar Sokkason's hearing, when I had
him brought before me for questioning. Perhaps
"questioning" is the wrong word, for even without recourse to physical torture, which I could
not bring myself to order in the case of a person
of such standing, and even of wealth, if indeed
there had been any wealth left in New Thule,
Einar Sokkason certainly felt the full sting of it.
As for me, I prepared myself through prayer, and
also through a penitence of sorts — although the
destitution which was now mine, living amongst

these people whose condition I shared, gave but scant occasion to inflict even more drastic privations on myself. What brew could I have drunk to mortify the flesh, when there was naught to drink but plain water rinsed of weeds? What concoction might I have made myself eat more foul than these scrapings from sea animal hides, seasoned with dead horses' hooves? In this climate, so frigid that even the birds had fled, the bear fat and seal lard (foods fundamentally and intrinsically ignoble) which my valiant sailors had brought back to us in the few casks that had escaped the massacre and pillage, were a greater delicacy to us than the sparrows of Aquitaine, which the languid Italians and the perverse Provençals call ortolan, or gardener bird. Yet we saved this grease and lard, scant as it was, for the children and the poorest of the poor. To enhance the gravity of my deportment, I wished that I might have donned the habit of my ministry, which in Your wisdom You had ordered me to take with me to the north of the world to affirm Your presence there as well as God's. Alas, I had given cope and surplice to the poor; the rest had been lost in the trials at sea and on the ice; in lieu of amice, alb, or dalmatic, of pallium, maniple, stole, or chasuble, I had on my back but a pitiful piecing of the outlawed capuches which I had had confiscated as donations to the church. It was appareled thus that I received Einar Sokkason, or, rather, that he was cast at my feet. Whether he had tried to resist when they came to seize him, or whether my sailors, although still worn out from their grievous expedition to the Land of No Homes, had vented upon him a forgivable fury, the Einar who came before me was but a shattered semblance of the human form. His lacerations would have been more congruous in the butcher's stall at the portals of the Nidaros cathedral, than they were with the reputation and authority which the man had enjoyed in the fjord that carried his name. Both ears had been torn off. One of his eyes was a cavernous hole; as for teeth, scarce to start with, there was but a single one left to prevent his tongue, swollen like that of a calf, from protruding from his mouth through cracked lips. My compassion had spared him the questioning, only to deliver him, willy-nilly, to the wrathful fists of my companions. My prisoner was in such a state that in cross-examining him I had no recourse but to provide the answers to the questions myself. This would have been quite an unorthodox manner of investigation, had not the Holy Spirit, whose presence is felt wherever the law is enforced and the truth is sought, decreed that I should already be cognizant of the whole affair; so that in the disclosure of the facts Einar might limit himself to responding to my pronouncements with a moan, or by shaking what was left of his head. It was in this mute manner that he did confess to the atrocities which had taken place at the farm of the Vales, at Undir Höfdi, situated not far from the abandoned church which, with her dependencies, had once in the darkness of time belonged to the cathedral of Gardar. If it is indeed true, as Your Grace has taught me, that the crime is to be judged by the motive, then the Tribunal of Heaven, where counsel, prosecutor and judge are one, will know that there were extenuating circumstances. If one takes into account that the pestilence running rampant in the Settlement coincided with the arrival of Jorsalafari and his monkey; and considering also that the villagers suspected this monkey to be the Beast of the Apocalypse, then it was not so farfetched for these rustic minds to conclude that exterminating the monkey would put an end to the pestilence. Whether it was through an excess of caution that they had massacred the monkey's peasant keepers, in an impulse to kill all things living around it in order to dispel the noxious miasmas; or whether it was the outcome of a brawl in which the farmers had tried to defend their strange pet, I could not determine, not even by lying to Einar that he might save his mortal frame (and not just his soul) if he would confess the truth. For I had resolved to have Einar put to death, no matter what he might do or say. I could not banish from my mind the fumes of that massacre, the still-steaming feces from loosened bowels, the blood spattered right up to the rafters, the corpses so horribly mutilated that they were unrecognizable; in lieu of being welcomed by the lost Christians whom we had journeyed to the ends of the earth to save, we had been met with that ghoulish vespers. In opting for such twisted severity, I also sought political advantage. I had come to the conclusion that under the rigors of such extreme poverty, there could not be two voices of authority in Gardar, one answering to the popular will, the other answering to Your Grace's bidding and the commandments of the Most High. When we had narrowly avoided a rebellion over the horse fights, I had sensed a weakening of the ancient alliance of the plow and the cross. Einar Sokkason had entirely failed in his duty of obedi-ence and his obligations as leader. Overly atten-tive to the people's grumbling, he had stubbornly opposed my strictest decrees and my harshest demands. Besides having been responsible for a terrible massacre, he had been guilty of the most unpardonable sin which a leader can commit: that of wanting to please . I had him decapitated on the beach, before the entire populace. His head was thrown to the wolves. The rest was given a Christian burial.

Chapter 7

NEITHER THE RESTORATION OF MY AUTHORITY following Einar Sokkasson's torture and execution, nor the eradication of the people's worst vices through the strictest application of justice, nor even the provisions stocked up through our efforts to promote a new zeal for agriculture, could prevent the winter from hitting us hard. The daytime cold was followed by an even worse freeze at night; it grew so bad that I heard people inveighing against God, and telling Him they would prefer the fires of hell.

Some went so far as to vow that they would resume their former sins if it would mean punishment by hellfire; for to roast in any fire would be a reward rather than a torment; some of them, in search of the most extreme crime, committed the sins of apostasy and infidelity by staging a perversion of the baptism, wherein they doused themselves in excrement while abjuring the name of God. I quickly packed these wretches off to the gallows, as much for their lack of judgment as for their lack of faith: for how could they hope to be punished for their apostasy by the very God Whom they repudiated? The peat, on which our lives depended, was running very low in all the households, despite the great quantities I had had them dig up and store before the autumn. None dared to venture beyond the village limits for fear that they would freeze to death, but if indeed anyone had gone as far as the peat fields, he would have found them frozen solid, so that it would have been impossible to dig the peat out of the rock-hard ground. The eyes froze in the sockets, drying up even the most justified tears.

Children died in the straw-lined wicker baskets
that were their cradles; administering the last
rites, I would catch a glimpse of their poor little
faces, all bloated and blue. It was yet a boon if
the parents had not used these pathetic cradles
to make a fire, sacrificing their children for a little
heat. All the food was frozen hard, so that even
after being mashed in their rustic mortars and
pestles, those who had lost their teeth were
unable to chew it, and it caused, in those who
still had a few teeth, a dreadful disorder of the
bowels. The dogs would fall on these excreta and
devour them ere they were cold. I had a number
of sheep and cows herded into the cathedral, so
that their warmth would save those whom poverty, bad luck or cruel neighbors had deprived of
shelter. I took the liberty of choosing to sleep
amongst these poor souls instead of in my own
quarters; thus was my charity recompensed with
the physical comfort my generous impulse had
provided to others. I was troubled that that
which was but the fulfillment of my mission
might be construed by some to be a calculated

stratagem. I toured the houses in person to pick
and choose the least frail of the infants, or those
that were the most deserving, and tucked them
beneath the muzzles of my cows, which cosseted
them with their breath. On Christmas Eve, when
the stars were so cold that the parishioners perished on their way to hearing Mass, one of these
children and the sturdiest of the cows replicated
the holy tableau of Bethlehem in the dim light of
the seal-oil lamp, while outside the wolves, waiting for the kill, howled at the foot of the glacier.

On the first days of spring, the publican
maid came to me on her knees to confess that she
was with child again. Having been delivered at
Candlemass of a still-born child, sired by a forni-
cator of her own race, she had, whether out of
innocence or perversity, lost no time in returning
deliberately to the same replenished state into
which she had been erstwhile coerced. I asked to
hear her confession. Emboldened by the authority
I have from God by leave of Your Grace, further-

more expecting that at the time when you read this report I will no longer be alive, and confident that the false report of an alleged scandal permits me to reveal it here, I prostrate myself at Your august feet, and entreat you to trust me rather than believe my lamentable penitent. At my urging her to tell me what had caused her present state, in her despair she had the audacity to protest that I myself was its author. I was quite prepared to excuse such a monstrous lie, in consideration of the terrible tribulations she had suffered, and the distress that these had caused her, by attributing it to her confused state of mind and disturbed memory, and consequently I absolved her forthwith; but she would not recant, and even went so far as to entreat me to admit to this sinful paternity; I gave her to understand that such a demand did not fit the scope of the confession, no matter what the substance of the case might be. She repeated her plea, throwing herself upon my bosom; she would have fallen to her knees before me if the sacrament which I was in the process of administering to her had not already required her to be kneeling before God. However, in order to find out the truth, it behooved me to delve into all the details, no matter how repugnant these might be; did not Your Grace and M. the Count of Ascoyne both teach me, withal, that God is all in the details? I beg leave of Your Grace, therefore, to recapitulate the sordid minutiae herewith. First I ordered the maiden to reveal to me with whom, and in what position, illicit or lawful, she had had amorous encounters since her lying-in; upon the understanding that when performed out of wedlock, even the lawful positions are a crime. She swore to me upon her unborn child that she had neither opened, nor lowered, nor torn off the miserable fur undergarment which covered her shameful parts to protect them from the cold, in the fashion of the maidens of her race, for any man excepting the one whom she alleged to be Your servant. As she spoke, she lifted up her ragged skirt, opening her legs wide, to show me the breechcloth she wore to hide that which she was now revealing, the sight of which, I must confess, did not fail to move me, notwithstanding the scum, the blood, and the stench of poverty which did desolate the intimacy of it. I asked her if she had not made one of those shameless hand gestures, delivering semen from her mouth to her most secret vestibule. To which she replied that I was the only man whom she might have accorded such a favor, if it were indeed one, and whom she might have permitted, furthermore, to relish a sweet tasting. I sought to impress on her what an abomination this sort of behavior was to Heaven, linking together four mortal sins: the sin of Onan, the sin of fellatio, the sin of lust and the sin of gluttony. She had the effrontery to claim she did not understand me, for, she said, what difference did it make to God, whether it be lust, semen spilled or swallowed, that it was all the same thing, and therefore ought not to be lumped together as justification for a manifold condemnation. In this equivocation, wherein I found not a trace of my poor girl's innocence, I did detect the work of the Evil One, who is as skilled at insinuating himself into the most unsophisticated souls with his cunning arguments, as he is at seducing the most worldly ones. I perceived the confusion by which the young publican was carried away, so that despite the enormity of her misdeeds, these might very well not arise to the level of sin. Next I questioned her about sodomy. I beg Your Grace to believe that in doing so I was not driven by curiosity, for like Yourself I am acquainted with the most extreme recesses of perversion, so that neither of us, no matter how piquant the spice, is ever inflamed by such revelations. She denied it vehemently. I suggested that perhaps there might be a mitigating circumstance in the error, and some propriety in the indecency, if, obliged to disrobe for a call of nature, she might have presented the portal of her *excreta* to some virile indiscretion. She persisted in her denials, made even more persuasive by her remarking, with reason, that such an encounter in and of itself could not possibly have caused her to be with child. It was futile to remind her that in a storm one port is as good as the next, and that a vessel which, through urgency, has grown storm-tossed, might in a moment of inattention very well make landfall in either one. She was so insistent in her allegations, invested her calumny with so many charms, and her accusation with such consistency, that she almost persuaded me to doubt my own innocence. To that end she even went so far as to make certain gestures which I fancied could be the very ones I did suspect her of; thus did the confession inspire the very sins from which it was intended to absolve her. She drew me into a dizzying confusion of hems and apertures which my ministry ought to have convinced her to keep hidden from the light. Your Grace, who knows men's failings and their weaknesses, will determine without hearing my confession whether I did indeed succumb, or had succumbed ere this day, in such a way that it might have led her to conceive hopes of maternity. I shall not try to justify myself, for it is not my place to vaunt my own virtue, having enough on my hands in prosecuting the vices of others. I do ask Your Grace nevertheless to try to picture the icy blackness of the winter we had just survived; the cold hearths deprived of peat, where the only warmth to be found was in the communal bed, and the only exercise was tossing and turning to assuage the insect bites and the hunger pangs of an empty stomach; nights when the fog rolling down from the frozen wastes, mingling with the exhalations of an icy sea, wormed its way through every nook and cranny, penetrating the body's most secluded intimacy and swaddling us in an all-enveloping shroud; but a welcome shroud withal, since it tempered the ferocity of the cold; we would miss the fog on nights yet far more terrible, when the harsh glare of the stars, and the hostile silence of the moon, flooded our petrified village with a light more unforgiving than darkness. On those nights, the wolves froze to death, as did the bears; we would chop them up with our hatchets the next morning. Your Grace will gauge if such wintry weather encouraged lechery, in asking for a little warmth in the rubbing and the rocking, as well as some release from the lethargic immobility to which we were condemned; or whether, on the contrary, this immobility and lethargy might inhibit even the caresses and other transports of love.

The next summer, besides being of such short duration that it seemed to be yearning for winter, and besides bringing back the mosquitoes and a new outbreak of the disease, now delivered to us a new set of afflictions.

As we worked ourselves near to death harvesting the meager fruits of a low and niggardly sun, dreading another winter as fearsome as the preceding one, a plague of caterpillars came upon us, swarming across fields and pastures and stripping down to the very ground our paltry crops and the grass not yet grown to hay. Some of the publicans, following the custom of their race, tried to eat them, but were punished for the ravenousness of their hunger by a thousand poisoned stingers that cover these insects like a coat of fur; so that the horror of their deaths reflected the ghastliness of the food that caused it; the poor wretches fled hither and thither, flailing their arms, gasping for air, their mouths and throats swollen with the venom, until they fell to the ground and lay there choking, seized with convulsions, whimpering mutely, a sound which made me think of fish being auctioned on the docks of Nidaros. Some tried to save themselves by casting themselves into the sea, meaning to relieve their agony by gulping the water, only to meet an icy death. These creatures swarmed right into the houses, the stables, and even the cathedral, coating the ground in a layer that squelched underfoot, spurting a thick kind of glue.

Chapter 8

ᴠ

BUT THE LORD'S GREENERY WAS NOT ALONE in feeling the brunt of His ire. Cattle, horses and pigs were infested with warble-boils; the affliction was so severe that no villager had seen the like in all living memory. It caused the malnourished animals to grow ever more emaciated, so that the season in which they should have filled out left many of them but walking skeletons. The poor animals, covered in abscesses oozing with a foul discharge, would stagger around twitching and shaking off great quantities of the vermin; we understood that these were but the seed from which would spring even greater multitudes of the grub which some of the publicans had mistaken for a delicacy. Thus did our wretched cattle, in trying to rid themselves of their torment, create another far worse. Their leather, riddled with a thousand holes, was quite useless, and the flesh so lean that we feasted on the smallest bones, sucking out their marrow, and gobbling down the eyes. As for the sheep, whose fleece prevented the moths from laying their eggs within the skin, the maggots invaded them through the nose, burrowing directly into their brains, where they dug their nests. The infested beasts would lurch about like drunken sailors, but the only ones to find this amusing were the children, for the rot would spoil the carcases ere the return of the cold weather gave us the chance to preserve them, since the sun was not hot enough to permit the meat to be dried and cured.

In the depths of winter, the publican maid gave birth to a son, whom she obstinately claimed was mine. The joys of becoming a mother had eclipsed the shame of unwed motherhood. There was no sign of a father, save the one she had designated in her allegations. Notwithstanding the scandal, I accepted by charity what I should have refused by rights. The gossip, and presently the grumblings of my flock, persuaded me to listen to my heart rather than my reason, and, contrary to the laws of nature and blood, I came to love this son whose paternity was imposed on me by rumor, rather than through the transports of the flesh. The child's baptism had to be a rushed affair, for fear that the cold, in curtailing its young life, would send it to Limbo, whereas at birth it was promised Paradise, whether or not it had been conceived in sin. We debated at length what to call it; we chose not to leave that decision to the godfather or godmother, on whom we had likewise been unable to agree. She wished to give the infant the name of its great-grandfather, Sorqaq, so skilled a bear hunter, she said, that his name was legend and his renown spread far and wide, from Undir Höfdi to the Land of No

Homes. She even told me, without convincing me, that he had crossed the High Country alone with his dogs, that vast tract of ice from which no one (save him) had ever returned. In the east he had discovered an unknown sea, frozen to its very depths, bristling with seals. I scoffed at this ancestor of hers and said he was a liar, for who might believe that seals could exist without water in which to swim under the ice? And furthermore, I said, did she not know, from her own people's history (since in bygone times when those animals were abundant around the Settlement, her people used to feast on them), that seals feed on fish? I added another objection: had she not heard how the great Sorqaq, of whom she spoke with such pride, had met his death? She confessed that upon returning from a fruitless hunt, and starving of hunger like his dogs, these had devoured him. His corpse had been found savagely torn to shreds, together with what remained of his sled and the bodies of his dogs, all yet unscathed, lying at the bottom of one the crevasses created by the thundering advance of the glacier which flows from the High Country down to the fjord. That Sorqaq, a hunter, had met such an ignominious death, I said, was a bad omen for anyone bearing his name. Albeit wholly ignorant of the system of lunatic beliefs which passes for religion on the part of the publicans, I had divined correctly: to these simple souls (if they do indeed have souls), the name's ill-starred history will bring ill luck to the wearer: in contrast, how ingenious is the device of our own martyrs, whose very misfortunes protect those who are placed under their patronage! I see this as another sign of the preeminence of the true faith. Thus was I successful in appealing to both the barbarian and the Christian in her —twin sources of the scant judgment she did possess. I imposed the name Einar, taking it upon myself to represent Your Grace in the role of the child's godfather, for surely the numerous fruitful commissions which You have granted me entitle me thereunto. Wherewith I did satisfy several worthy requirements: Einar, Your Grace's spiritual nephew and godson;

Einar, for he was born in Einarsfjord; and Einar, in whom the heresies of a dark and murky past would be blotted out by the light which Your Grace casts to the confines of his archdiocese. It did, certainly, give me pause to remember that it was also the name of Einar Sokkason, whose head I had ordered chopped off for his crimes; but at least he was a Christian sinner, namesake and kin to Your Grace, who, sadly, was led astray by a petulant reading of the Apocalypse.

To show that I was worthy of the mother's devotion, I had an obligation to provide for her, as publican custom dictated. As for the child, it received enough milk, for she suckled it for three years: as with all the womenfolk of her race, her breasts were prodigiously fertile. They tell me that some sons sucked at their mother's breast until they were of bear-hunting age. I was not able to verify such a wonder with my own eyes, yet I was not insensible to the wisdom of Providence in this regard: the paltry foods, insufficient and rotten, which these people do manage to wring from a stinting nature, are more likely to kill a child than to keep it alive; mother's milk shields them from such. I observed that it also had another consequence: suckling their young does not dispose the females to become pregnant again, or even prevents them entirely from it; child-bearing ceases; if it were not so, these wretched souls would be constrained, for an excess of mouths to feed, to expose and abandon many more newborns — of which crime I have already informed Your Grace. It was further imperative, for the sake of the young publican's milk, that her blood be enriched with meat and fish. I had to go out hunting and fishing, employing the methods of these barbarians, though I must say these were far below the dignity and unction of a person of my position, more congruent to the cloth than to animal hides, and more adept at wielding the ostensorium than the harpoon.

The day approached when we would set sail for the return to the Mother Country. I suffered a thousand torments of the soul, torn between the obligation to report back to you on my mission, and seek help for these people who find themselves in such dire straits, and the sense of duty which might have constrained me to remain among them and share in their final days. On the one hand, I feared that my departure might be construed as flight attributable to cowardice; on the other, was it truly so Christian to court death, even to keep others company, and, in sustaining my flock with the Word, to renounce saving them in the deed? During the lengthy preparations for our voyage, I had all the time to decide whether it were more honorable to endure the daily increase of a suffering leading inexorably to death, and drown out the moans of the people under a torrent of prayers; or to brave instead the perils of the open seas. Ere I made my final decision, I ordered that our ship be readied down to the minutest detail; since she had been disassembled for being hauled over the ice, I instructed the boatswain and the Captain to undertake a thorough inspection and to scrutinize every joint, even if it meant removing all interior planking and equipment in order to collect the necessary materials wherewith to fashion clinkers and braces; to clean, scrape, and drain the wood by chipping off the rotted parts and by stripping it of the weeds and shellfish which are a ship's leprosy; finally to caulk every crack, fissure, chink and cleft with moss dipped in the last drop of pitch that we possessed (leading me to observe that pitch, and even tallow, were more precious to us than gold, of little consequence when it comes to a sailor's survival, since neither doubloons nor ducats will pay for calm waves or tranquil winds.) This in turn led to a dispute with my people over the supplies needed to outfit the ship, foremost the strife over cordage. Wear and tear, and the brown rot brought about by seawater, which never dries, had cost me a shortfall of some twenty fathoms of rope. I was obliged to conduct a search of all the houses myself, poking in every nook and cranny in order to find a sufficient length, since the villagers refused to surrender it willingly to me. I was forced to employ the

cross, which I had to hold before me like St. John
Chrysostom when he confronted the Empress
Eudoxia, in order to have them open their doors
to me, that is, those which could still be called
doors, since many of their thresholds were shield-
ed by naught but some flaps of leather, or bales of
hay too rotted to serve as cattle feed. The repair
of The Short Serpent's square sail was likewise
subject to heated debate with my flock. No matter how I might argue that it was so threadbare
that one could see the daylight through it, and
that, worn out by the years and the miles traveled, it was likely to be ripped to shreds in the
first breath of wind, they would bitterly respond
that my sail was not worth the sacrifice of the
scant warmth which the orphan, the widow, or
the sick could obtain from a cloth of the required
weight; or that, should I choose to employ animal
skins instead, like the monks who, legend has it,
sailed hither all the way from foggy Hibernia, I
would be depriving the people of the wherewith-
al to protect themselves from the terrible winds
blasting down from the High Country. As for my

intention to take aboard a month's provisions as a precaution, accounting for windless days as well as contrary winds and tempests, I should not even dream of doing so; I would have to do my own foraging in the sea for food for my sailors, they said; as for myself, I always had the option of sacrificing my own life, in the name of that Christ whom I claimed to represent. Turning a deaf ear to such sanctimonious talk, I adopted the commendable stratagem of betaking myself to the villagers to beg for grain, casks of salted herring, eggs preserved in ash and rancid seal-lard, whilst pushing along before me the young publican and her child, whose father I openly claimed to be, at least for the nonce; and, since I declared it was my intention to take the child aboard with me, as well as its mother, I did not imagine that my flock would condemn them both to die of starvation.

Chapter 9

STRANGE TO THINK HOW MY LITTLE FLOCK turned against me, though it was in order to save them that I was abandoning the shelter which the cathedral provided me, and the modest convenience of my hovel there, which I shared with the young publican maid, and seeing that it was for love of them that I was going to confront the atrocities of a frigid sea. Their furor increased as my preparations proceeded. I had thought that I could have the ship pulled up on shore, so that it might be worked on with ease without imperiling its security. But the general ill will constrained me to post armed men to guard the ship day and night. The caulking, the joinery and the loading were done within a bulwark of shields and under the watchful eyes of the archers. We slept aboard The Short Serpent, thus fortified against the very people she was preparing to rescue. Nor did we quite manage to evade the stones hurled at us by the children, spurred on by their parents; and neither did The Short Serpent escape some arson attempts, in the form of blazing clumps of peat catapulted at it, thereby frittering away a goodly amount of fuel which, when the cold set in again, might have saved several newborns. I did manifest to God my grief at seeing myself so badly repaid and so badly misunderstood. But there was even worse to come. At dawning of the day of our departure, when The Short Serpent, pushed by the crew, started her descent toward the sea, the young publican female, whom I had invited to come with us according to our mutual agreement, suddenly refused to climb on board and held out her son to me as if tendering a monstrance. I had barely taken the child in my arms when the ship's prow hit the water and the boatswain gave the measure for the first strokes of the oar. That was when, to my horror, I beheld the crowd assembled upon the beach stoning to death that same Avarana whom, she declared with her last breath, I had loved so dearly.

Chapter 10

ᚹ

ᚺ E DECIDED THAT IT WAS TIME TO PRE-
PARE *for his return, not because he had accom-
plished his mission — he was far from it, and
besides, was it even still possible? — but because
of the settlers' increasing hostility. It had started
with the dumping of offal and excrement at the
cathedral door in the night. In and of itself, a
rubbish pile close to the home was not necessar-
ily a sign of derision. Nor was it simply a display
of filthy habits. On the contrary, in prosperous
times, or what was remembered as such, that is
to say, before the big freeze, the farms had prided*

themselves on their dunghills, whose most nutritious ingredients, notably the human manure, were used to fertilize the fields and pastures. However, in light of its divine mission, the cathedral and its environs were expected to remain immaculate, notwithstanding the adjacent animal sheds. The Bishop understood, and immediately perceived that there was some ill feeling towards him. Soon he began having trouble obtaining provisions, whereas previously the farmers had not stinted in their generosity, providing him with an extraordinary largesse in view of the decline of every kind of agriculture and the reigning famine. Next he noticed that the parishioners were staying away from the Mass. During Holy Week and Easter, when in other years the cathedral would have been filled, only a handful of believers showed up, largely women, crowded into the back of the nave, timidly mumbling the responses. He spotted several bared black heads amongst the blond tresses escaping from ragged headdresses. At the end of the service it was customary for the faithful to congregate in the chancel alcove used as sacristy in order to receive the Bishop's blessing. In lieu of doing so, the faithful now turned on their heels as soon as the Mass was over and scampered for the icy road. Some time after this, Avarana returned carrying water with her face cut open by a rock. "Someone has been very frightened, someone could have wept with the pain, if she knew how to weep like your kind," she told the Bishop in her people's characteristically oblique manner. Avarana never wept. But her mouth, with the port-wine stain mark, was trembling, in contrast to her impassive face. The Bishop consoled her as best he could. He decided that he would post two armed sailors to stand guard at the cathedral.

The provisioning of The Short Serpent for a lengthy crossing was a constant point of contention between the prelate and the settlers. Both the practical furnishings, ropes, sailcloth, batting and pitch for the caulking, as well as the provisions, were bitterly haggled over. The Bishop was hoping for a crossing of ten days; but, taking into account any becalmed waters, head winds and bad weather, he had given himself a target of a month of rations for the entire crew. He was far from reaching that goal.

With the Captain and boatswain he drew up an inventory of what was lacking. They were short at least fifty pounds of barley flour, two casks of salted fish and six barrels of seal-lard. As for the last item, the Bishop could be quite sure that its shortage had to be due to the villagers' ill will, since, for the first time in years, the month of May had seen the return of the seals, and, notwithstanding the general fatigue and dearth of weapons, there had been a successful cull. The three men debated the consequences. They were brought to the conclusion that the rations would have to be reduced, and that they would have to cut back on the extra margin they had left for the contingency of weak or contrary winds. The crew itself, already four men short and numbering several amputees, could not be trimmed any further. The Bishop would have been loath to do so in any case, for reasons of shipboard morale. He deter-

mined that he would have to leave Avarana
behind instead.

At the departure, as *The Short Serpent* was
rolling down to the sea on a bed of round boulders slicked down with seal-tar, the Bishop
pushed the young woman off the boat as she tried
to climb aboard with her child in her arms. He
seized the little boy, swung him across the boards,
laid him down on the deck, and, turning back
toward Avarana, gave her a hard shove that
made her fall in the water. Avarana got to her
feet and clung to the ship, pleading to be given
back her son. The helmsman, who held aloft the
rudder-oar so that it would not scrape over the
bottom, sought the Captain's order with a wink:
the Captain nodded. The helmsman then took a
knife from his belt and hacked off one of
Avarana's fingers. This made her let go; slowly,
on her knees, she made her way back to the shore,
tinting the icy water crimson with her blood.
Holding her mutilated hand high in the air, she
ran along the stony beach toward the assembled
crowd, which was shouting imprecations after

The Short Serpent, her master and her crew. A boy threw a stone at Avarana, crushing her nose. She fell. A hailstorm of stones and pebbles came raining down on her. Methodically, and with an eerie calm, the villagers proceeded to stone her to death, crying "Bishop's whore!" until her limp body, stretched out on the bloodied rocks, moved no more.